D0414039

DEFINITELY DAISY

Daisy Dares

Collect all Daisy's adventures:

Watch Out, Daisy
Not Again, Daisy
Daisy Dares

Other series by Jenny Oldfield:

Totally Tom
The Wilde Family
My Little Life
Home Farm Twins
Horses of Half Moon Ranch

DEFINITELY DAISY

Daisy Dares

Jenny Oldfield

Hodder
Children's
Books

A division of Hodder Headline Limited

'With special thanks to the pupils of
St Mary's C of E School. Boston Spa'

Text copyright © 2005 Jenny Oldfield
Illustrations copyright © 2001 Lauren Child

First published in Great Britain in 2005
by Hodder Children's Books

The right of Jenny Oldfield to be identified as the Author of
This Work has been asserted by her in accordance with the
Copyright, Designs and Patents Act 1988.

2 4 6 8 10 9 7 5 3 1

All rights reserved. Apart from any use permitted under UK copyright law,
this publication may only be reproduced, stored or transmitted, in any
form, or by any means with prior permission in writing of the publishers or
in the case of reprographic production in accordance with the terms of
licences issued by the Copyright Licensing Agency and may not be
otherwise circulated in any form of binding or cover other than that in
which it is published and without a similar condition being imposed on
the subsequent purchaser.

All characters in this publication are fictitious and any
resemblance to real persons, living or dead,
is purely coincidental.

A Catalogue record for this book is available from
the British Library

ISBN 0 340 88141 0

Typeset by Tracey Hurst

Printed and bound in Great Britain by
Bookmarque Ltd, Croydon, Surrey

The paper and board used in this paperback by Hodder Children's Books
are natural recyclable products made from wood grown in sustainable
forests. The manufacturing processes conform to the environmental
regulations of the country of origin.

Hodder Children's Books
a division of Hodder Headline Ltd
338 Euston Road
London NW1 3BH

One

'*Brm-brrm-brrm!*' Daisy Morelli made racing-car noises with her lips.

'Is it wise to let her do this?' her mum asked her dad, hanging on tight to Daisy's football.

'*B-b-brugh!*' Daisy made like a horse. She cantered round the kitchen of the Pizza Palazzo. '*Neigh!*'

Gianni Morelli shrugged. He slapped pizza dough on to a floured board. 'With Daisy, nothing is wise.'

Daisy screeched to a halt. 'Hey!' she objected.

'Just kidding,' her dad said. *Slap-slap* with the dough. Clouds of white flour rose from the board.

'But is it safe?' her mum, Angie, insisted. 'I mean,

isn't letting Daisy loose with a football in a busy park on a Sunday afternoon just asking for trouble?'

Daisy trotted to Gianni's side. 'I'm playing in the Junior Inter-Schools Cup Final tomorrow. Me and Jimmy have to train,' she pointed out, as if that made everything OK.

Sprinkling mushrooms on to the pizza base, he nodded. 'You'll stay in the park?'

'Yep.' With her fingers crossed behind her back, Daisy knew this promise didn't count. So if, for instance, the football went over a wall into someone's garden, they'd be able to climb over and fetch it. Or if they wanted to do some circuit training round the shops...

'You don't be nasty to little old ladies with dogs?'

'Nope.' Most times, she would have corrected her Italian dad's bad grammar, but today she simply looked up at him with what she hoped was an angelic smile.

On went the mountain of grated cheddar and a sprinkling of parmesan. There was a blast of heat as Gianni opened the oven and slid the pizza inside. 'OK, go!' he told her.

'*Brrrrm!*' Back in racing driver mode, Daisy grabbed the ball from her mum and made for the door.

'Don't get into trouble, and be back in half an hour!' Angie called.

'*Neeyah!*' A screech of brakes. Daisy raced across the restaurant.

'Wear your old trainers!'

Zoom! Fifty miles per hour through the front door.

'Don't get dirty!'

Her mum's voice faded behind her. Daisy was out on the pavement in her shiny new trainers, speeding down towards Jimmy's house. '*Huh!*' she thought out loud. '*That last bit doesn't make any sense. How can you practise your penalty kicks and go in for the tackle without getting covered in mud?*'

'Who-oh-oah!' Jimmy said.

'Eeeeagh!' Daisy screeched to a halt.

Her best friend had stepped out from the alley beside his house wearing a blue and white Steelers woolly hat pulled down over his eyebrows and a Steelers' scarf wrapped around his mouth in what he hoped was a cunning disguise.

'You're gonna be boiling hot in them, Jimmy Black,' Daisy pointed out, glancing up at the bright blue sky.

'How did you know it was me?' a disappointed Jimmy asked.

Daisy tutted. 'You were only coming out of your own house dressed in the scarf and hat you always wear, dummy!' She grabbed the end of his scarf and tugged. 'It's not winter any more, in case you didn't know.'

It was spring. The school soccer team had just had their best season ever. And now, with luck, they were about to win the Junior Inter-Schools Cup.

'You look stupid anyway,' Jimmy told her, getting his own back. 'Button nose, big mouth, messy hair...'

'Yeah, yeah. Let's go!' she decided. Her mum had given her half an hour – they'd better make the most of it.

'Where to?'

'The park.'

Jimmy nodded. 'Race you!' he said.

'Hmm!' Daisy frowned at the floppy remains of her white plastic ball.

She'd just taken her third penalty kick, with Jimmy crouched in goal, when Winona Jones's pesky poodle had pounced.

'Woof-raagh-wumph!' Then... Psssss! Poodles might look curly and namby-pamby, but their teeth were well sharp.

Daisy had watched her ball deflate. It sat sadly on a lump of mud. Then Jimmy had thrown himself at it and sprawled on top.

Pssssss!

'Gerroff!' Daisy had cried, rummaging under the

goalie to rescue her ball. Too late. It was flat as a pancake.

'It wasn't Mimi's fault!' Winona jumped in, scooping up her precious pet.

'You shouldn't have been kicking the silly thing while we were walking by!' Winona tossed her blonde curls back from her face. 'Mimi thought you wanted her to join in.'

'Hm,' Daisy grunted.

'"Hm!" Is that all you can say?' Winona challenged, setting her poodle back on its feet. Mimi yapped and jumped up at the ball.

Daisy glared at Winona – at the glossy curls, the smarmy face, the crisp white top and trendy, matching cut-off trousers.

'Just leave it, OK!' Jimmy whispered, pulling at the back of Daisy's T-shirt.

'My b-b-ball!' she spluttered.

Winona sniffed. 'Here, Mimi!' she called in her high-pitched voice. 'Come away from Daisy. She's all dirty!'

Daisy stared at the sad-looking, flattened object in her hands. Her own heroic saves had left her covered in mud. She was sweaty, her dark hair was sticking to her forehead, and she was breathing hard.

'You sound like a walrus,' Winona giggled, turning to walk away. 'And, guess what, you look like one too!'

That was it. Ms Neat 'n' Petite was not going to get away with that! 'Hold this,' Daisy ordered Jimmy. She handed him the ball, took a deep breath...and launched herself at Winona.

'We said, don't get into trouble!' Daisy's mum stood with her hand on one hip, balancing baby Mia on the other.

'I stayed in the park, didn't I? And I wasn't horrible to any old ladies.' Daisy thought her mum was being a teensy bit tough.

OK, so Winona's mum had shown up at Pizza Palazzo and waved Winona's mud-caked cut-offs in their faces, in front of all their customers. 'These are brand new trousers!' she'd screeched. 'They cost twenty-five pounds!'

And OK, maybe Daisy had overdone the getting-her-own-back bit when she'd rugby tackled Winona. But it had been spur of the moment, and the urge had just welled up inside her until she couldn't speak and all she could do was launch herself...

'Put Winona's trousers in the washing machine,' Daisy's mum ordered grimly. 'If they don't come clean, I'm going to buy her a new pair and stop your pocket money until they're paid for!'

'Grug!' Mia said, then wiggled her bare, chubby toes.

'Their dog wrecked my ball!' Daisy grumbled. 'Why don't you make them pay for that?'

'Daisy – trousers – washing machine!' Angie warned.

'Not fair!' Winona-Stupid-Jones had brought Jimmy and Daisy's valuable training session to a full stop. And it was the final tomorrow – their big day! 'I bet this doesn't happen at Highfield training ground!' she grumbled.

'Gruggle-gug-groo!' Mia gurgled.

'That poodle should be kept on a lead,' Daisy muttered, heading for the kitchen and stuffing Winona's cut-offs into the machine. 'It's vicious.

I'm gonna phone the RSPC-wotsits.'

She tipped in soap powder, pressed buttons, listened to the first swish and whir of the super-hot cycle, then went to flop down in front of the telly.

Pink? Herbie squeaked.

He squatted on Daisy's pillow, his one beady eye staring at her.

'Yeah, bright pink,' Daisy explained. 'They started off white, but there was one of Dad's red socks hidden in the bottom of the machine, so when I took them out, the trousers had gone pink.' She groaned, sighed, then squidged Herbie into a more comfy position for the night.

How much is that going to cost you? Herbie asked without opening his mouth.

(So, everyone else thought Herbie was just this squashed, half-bald, beanie-babe hamster with one eye missing, but to Daisy he was the only person in the house worth talking to.)

'Twenty-five,' she sighed.

Twenty-five pence? Herbie queried.

'No, twenty-five quid!'

Wow!

'Yeah, wow!'

After this there was nothing left to say. Herbie and Daisy lay in the dark, thinking.

'Herbie?' she began after a long silence.

Yep?

Daisy snuggled him closer to her cheek. 'I can't get to sleep.'

Why not? Are you still thinking about Ms Neat and Petite?

'No. I've got butterflies.'

Car headlights raked over the ceiling. In the distance, a police siren wailed.

'About tomorrow,' she confessed. 'It's the Cup Final. I'm dead nervous.'

Herbie left a short pause. *Don't worry, you'll be fine,* he said sleepily.

'What if I fall over the ball and look like an idiot? Or I could miss an open goal, or get sent off!' With the butterflies turning into a herd of cows trampling inside her stomach, Daisy pictured all the disasters that might happen. 'In front of the whole school!' she whined.

There was silence from the one-eyed rodent.

'Herbie?' Daisy whispered.

Z-z-z-z!

He was fast asleep.

Two

And it's Woodbridge Road Juniors 2, Marshway Juniors 2, with one minute to go! The referee is looking at his watch. It seems like this match is heading into extra time...

Daisy tossed and turned on her pillow, squidging Herbie into a flattened version of his chubby self. The hamster slept on.

But wait! Black has got the ball and is taking it into the Marshway half. Morelli's with him, but is she offside?
No, the linesman hasn't raised his flag. Morelli's onside, and Black passes to her in the goalmouth. Morelli body-

swerves two Marshway defenders, but she still has one to beat. The goalie crouches ready…can Morelli get through? She flicks the ball with her left foot, past the full back, and now there's only the goalie between her and Woodbridge's dream of glory…

She shoots! It's in the net! Morelli leaps in the air. The whistle blows. Woodbridge have won the Cup!

'Yeah!' Daisy shot up in bed, her heart pounding. 'We did it!' she cried.

She looked around her room in the dim dawn light.

'You OK?' her dad asked, peering round the edge of her door, his black hair sticking up like a spiky nest.

'What? Uh – yes,' Daisy mumbled, dragging Herbie out from the neck of her pyjamas.

'We heard you shout. You have bad dream, my Daisy?'

Daisy shook her head, recalling the moment when her right foot had contacted the heavy ball, and *thud!*, it had shot like a cannon ball into the back of the net. 'No, it was a good dream,' she sighed. 'I scored a goal and we won the Junior Inter-Schools Cup!'

'Ah!' Gianni rubbed his stubbly chin, then yawned. 'Is great. Good sign for later, huh?'

Daisy grinned, plumped Herbie up and tucked him back under the duvet.

'Now stop being Robbie Exley and go back to sleep,'

her dad said, shuffling off to bed.

And it's Woodbridge Road Juniors 2, Marshway Juniors 2, with one minute to go!

Daisy stared out of the window at the empty playing field. Miss Ambler rambled on about Norman helmets and spears.

Adam Bell, the Marshway centre, picks up the loose ball. Oh my, that was a bad mistake by Jimmy Black, and it's given Bell a chance in the Woodbridge box! The goalie's out of position, and now there's only Morelli between the Marshway attacker and the goal. Can she put in the necessary tackle?

She goes in with both feet, but she's got the girl, not the ball. Bell goes down. Well, that was one of the worst fouls I've seen in the schools league this season – a total disgrace! The ref blows his whistle. It's a penalty for Marshway, and a deserved sending-off for Morelli. And this is the big chance for Marshway to come out on top…

'Daisy?' Miss Ambler barked.

'Uh – huh – wha'?' She jumped as her mate Leonie dug her in the ribs.

'I said, who led the Norman army when they invaded Britain?' the teacher repeated.

'Phuh.' Daisy let out a gloomy breath then gave a shrug. The disgrace of giving away a vital penalty, even in her own private dream world, stayed with her. It felt like being punched in the stomach and having all the air knocked out of you.

'Miss Ambler, I know!' Winona's hand shot up. 'Miss, it was William the Conqueror!'

'Well done, Winona.' The teacher came up to Daisy's desk. Her droopy skirt brushed Daisy's leg. 'Daisy, can you tell me why your *Meet The Normans!* book is still closed instead of being open at page ten? And why haven't you filled in the section on the worksheet about Norman helmets?'

Daisy frowned.

Once more Winona came in with the answer. 'Miss, she wasn't listening. I saw her staring out of the window…'

'Yes, thank you, Winona dear. Daisy, you're going to make a mess of this whole project if you don't pay attention.'

'Yes miss. Sorry miss.' Slumped over her book, Daisy couldn't lose the dread of letting her team down. You could take away a whole year's pocket money, put her in detention after school, even sling her in a dark dungeon and give her medieval torture, but to Daisy there was nothing worse than giving away a penalty.

'Don't worry, you'll be fine,' Leonie whispered to her after Rambler Ambler had wandered off. Leonie was a mind reader – the cleverest girl in the class. Nathan Moss was the cleverest boy, but he was only interested in collecting bus tickets and keeping pet spiders.

Daisy gave Leonie a weak smile.

'It's a big match. You're bound to be nervous,' Leonie hissed. 'Me too. Look, my hand's trembling.'

'I'm scared stiff!' Daisy admitted in a faint voice.

'Daisy Morelli, I won't tell you again!' Miss Ambler squeaked from the front of the class, underneath a wall chart of the Bayeux Tapestry.

'Either you concentrate, or I put you outside in the corridor until you come to your senses!'

Daisy's eyes lit up. Now that was the sort of sending-off she definitely liked the sound of!

'Daisy Morelli, what are you doing out here?' The Headteacher, Mrs Waymann, paused in the corridor. She glared at Daisy with raised eyebrows. A rose-scented cloud wafted down. 'No, don't tell me. Let me guess. You spilled paint over Maya? You tripped over Jared's bag? You broke Nathan's glasses?'

'No!' Daisy said in an offended voice.

Mrs Waymann sighed. 'So, Daisy, what unlooked-for disaster has befallen you on this particular occasion?'

Daisy stared. She hadn't a clue what Waymann meant.

The arched eyebrows twitched into a frown. 'Oh never mind. Just don't let it happen again!' Mrs Waymann snapped, patting the side of her hairdo and sailing on in her perfumed cloud.

'Huh, I might have known,' Bernie King grunted as he stamped by.

Daisy was still standing in the corridor, beginning to feel hungry, while Winona and the others drew pictures of King Harold getting shot in the eye by an arrow.

The caretaker's keys jangled from his belt. His stubbly hair bristled as he towered over Daisy. 'If I had a pound for every time you got into bother, Daisy Disaster Morelli, I'd be a rich man!'

Daisy bit her tongue and sulked big-style.

'So what is it this time? Have you let the hamster out of its cage again? Or busted the nozzle in the girls' showers by any chance?'

How come I have this name for getting into trouble? Daisy wanted to know. *OK, so bad things happened, but they weren't my fault. Well, hardly ever.* She glowered up at Bernie.

Luckily he had tables and chairs to set out in the hall, ready for lunch, so he stomped on. 'Yes, I'd be a millionaire,' he chuntered, pleased at his own little joke.

'How are you feeling, Daisy?' Jimmy asked during the last lesson of the day.

It was art. They were making spring flowers out of coloured tissue paper and gluing them on to a frieze.

'Shaking like a leaf,' Daisy replied. Her daffodil petals were all wonky.

'Ha-ha-ha!' Jimmy laughed feebly, pointing to Daisy's wobbly flower. 'Like a leaf, or like a petal, ha-ha!'

'Leave it out, Jimmy,' Leonie groaned. 'It's bad enough already!'

Nerves were getting to them all. There was only half an hour to go before kick-off, and Jimmy was laughing at nothing, Leonie was telling everyone off, while Daisy had somehow managed to get glue in her hair.

'Very nice, Winona,' Miss Ambler trilled from halfway up the stepladder when the class swot handed her a perfect specimen of a primrose to stick on the wall.

'Very nice, Winona!' Daisy, Jimmy and Leonie echoed.

Winona ignored them, swishing by to start work on a bright pink tulip.

'Yuck!' Daisy sighed, trying to get the glue out of her locks but only making it worse.

'Don't worry, it'll wash out,' Nathan said. 'It's water-based PVA. And of course, solvents are not even allowed in the building. However, the best thing for this type of work would be an aerosol can of spray-mount.'

Daisy stopped mid-fiddle. 'Wow, Nathan,' she said flatly.

'No need to be sarcastic.' *Snip-snip*, Nathan cut out

the exact shape of a daisy petal, one and a half centimetres from top to bottom.

'Are you coming to the match?' Winona asked the brain box in a sing-song voice.

Daisy, Jimmy and Leonie suddenly tuned in.

'Are you?' Nathan checked with Winona.

'Of course. I'm serving the oranges at half-time. It's a big match, you ought to show support for the school.'

Nathan snipped and sniffed. 'Might do,' he muttered.

'B-b-but!' Jimmy gasped.

'You don't even know the rules of football!' Daisy cried. Nathan had never been near a soccer touchline in his entire geeky life.

'Yes, I do.' *Snip.* 'Test me.'

'OK, how do you decide when a player's offside?'

'Easy. There has to be at least one defender plus the goalkeeper between the ball and the goalposts when -'

'Daisy, look at you, you're a disgrace!' Miss Ambler sighed from the top of her stepladder before Nathan could quote the whole FA rulebook. 'You've got glue all over you. Go to the cloakroom this minute and wash it off!'

Three

The whole school was there, both staff and pupils.

The opposition had set off early from Marshway Junior School in the centre of town, and arrived at Woodbridge Road just as the final bell rang. Their sports teacher leaped out of the mini-bus in a bright red tracksuit and quickly ordered his team into the gym changing rooms.

'Wow, they look tall!' the Woodbridge supporters gasped. 'Did you see the kid with the ponytail? And what about the girl who was at least six foot two!'

'Yeah, she's their captain. She mashes anyone who gets in her way!'

Daisy and the rest of the team tried not to listen. They'd sprinted to their own changing room for the team talk from their coach, Mr Wright.

'...Defenders, never take your eye off your opponent. Mark him or her for every second of the game. Attackers, make space up front, catch their defence off-guard, seize your chances...'

At last they'd changed into their white strip with the blue stripes down the sleeves, they'd laced up their boots and trotted on to the pitch.

And now everyone was cheering. There was a sea of faces along the touchline and behind the goals. The referee strode out dressed all in black, with a silver whistle hanging around his neck.

Daisy felt the eyes of the crowd bore into her. She stood in line at the centre of the pitch while their captain, Jared Ikram, called 'Heads!' and the coin came down tails.

That gave Marshway the right to kick off, making the Woodbridge players scurry back to defend their goalmouth. As she ran, Daisy's legs felt stiff and her throat was dry.

'Come on the Whites!' the crowd roared.

'Up the Reds!' came the thinner cry from the visiting fans.

The kid with the ponytail kicked the ball to Adam Bell, the six-foot-two Marshway centre and team captain. She passed it short and Daisy dived in to intercept, collecting the ball with her left foot and dribbling clear of her opponent.

'Nice one, Daisy!' Leonie cried, racing up the right wing.

She took the ball twenty yards up the pitch, dodging and diving, ducking and weaving.

'Pass to me!' Jimmy yelled, running clear on her left.

Daisy flicked the ball with the inside of her right foot, found Jimmy and let him sprint on.

Better! she breathed. She'd had her first touch – the feel of the ball against her boot, the sound of the soft, reassuring thud as she'd passed it to Jimmy. Now it didn't seem as if the crowd was pressing in on her and her legs felt looser. She raced forward, level with Jimmy, with Leonie and Jared spear-heading the attack...

'Foul!' the Woodbridge supporters yelled when a burly Marshway attacker felled their goalie with a rough charge. Kyle picked himself up and claimed a free kick.

'Send him off!' Bernie King roared from the touchline. 'Referee, show him the red card!'

It was almost half-time and the score was still nil – nil. A thin drizzle had begun to fall.

The ref gave the Marshway player a telling-off.

'You OK?' Daisy asked Kyle. She lined the ball up

ready to take the free kick, planning to make it soar over the line of Marshway defenders and find Jared halfway up the pitch.

Kyle gave a dazed nod and retreated to his goalmouth.

Now! Daisy prayed. *Make this a good one!* If she could just raise the ball and bend it to the left, judge it exactly…

Five steps back, take a deep breath, blink, open eyes and charge. *Whumph!* She made contact and belted the ball high over the defenders' heads. It arched through the air, swerved slightly, found Jared on the centre line.

The crowd cheered. Jared flew with the ball on a solo run. He beat two defenders, aimed and fired.

Zoom!

The Marshway goalie dived and missed.

Zap! The ball was in the back of the net.

'One – nil, one – nil!' It was half-time and the Woodbridge fans were wild with joy.

'Excellent free kick!' Leonie told Daisy as they each took extra slices of orange from Winona's plate.

'Nathan, we've run out of oranges!' Winona piped, dressed up in a shiny lilac tracksuit and white trainers. 'Go and ask Miss Ambler for more!'

Nathan scowled but scurried to do as he was told.

Sucking the last drop of juice out of her fourth slice, Daisy noted that Nathan had shown up after all. Hmm, how on Earth had Ms Bossy-Boots persuaded him to come, she wondered.

'Teamwork!' Mr Wright was insisting. 'We've seen plenty of individual effort in the first half, but now what we need to see is you all working as a team!'

Across the pitch, the Marshway coach was in a huddle with his players. The rain was falling steadily.

On the touchline, Mrs Waymann sheltered under a purple umbrella, surrounded by teachers and parents. Meanwhile, Bernie King, followed by his waddling bulldog, Fat Lennox, checked the pitch for bumps and dents.

'This rain is making things a bit dodgy,' he

reported to anybody who would listen. 'These kids could break a leg on the greasy surface!'

'*Grrr!*' Lennox agreed, his jowls drooping gloomily.

But nothing could dent the confidence of the home team with their one-goal lead.

One all.

It was ten minutes into the second half and Marshway had pulled level with a shot from just inside the penalty box.

Kyle's reaction had been a shade slower than usual, the ball had rolled underneath his body and trickled into the net.

'Come on the Reds!' the visitors had screamed. Two kids had invaded the pitch and been shooed off by Bernie King.

Two – one to Marshway.

Ponytail Kid had held on to the ball during a scramble in front of the goalmouth, then bundled it over the line.

Daisy had skidded and flopped down into the mud, thudding into Jimmy, who had been dragged off the ball and shoved to one side by two Marshway attackers.

'Foul!' they'd cried, leaping to their feet and appealing to the ref. 'Free kick!'

'Goal!' he'd insisted.

'You sure you're OK, Kyle?' Daisy checked as he slowly went to gather the ball from the back of the net. Their goalie frowned and nodded.

Two all!

Superstar Leonie had scored the equaliser.

'Swing low, sweet chariot!' Woodbridge fans sang at the top of their voices.

'Ten minutes to go!' Jimmy hissed at Daisy as a Marshway attacker lost the ball in a fair tackle and flung himself to the ground, claiming a penalty.

'Play on,' the referee ordered.

The ball came to Daisy, who niftily sped down the centre with Jimmy alongside. Her legs going like engine pistons, she powered her way past a defender, faked a pass to Jimmy but hung on to the ball and flicked it to Jared instead.

'Nice move!' Mr Wright yelled from the touchline. 'Shoot, Jared, shoot!'

Three – two.

Jared had blasted the ball past the Marshway goalie.

Five minutes to go, plus three of extra time.

'Sir, what's up with Kyle?' voices from the crowd called.

The Woodbridge goalkeeper had wandered out of his goalmouth and was staggering towards the touchline.

'Get back in goal, Kyle!'

'What's the matter!'

'Sir, he's fainted!'

Seeing what was going on out of the corner of her eye, Leonie quickly tapped the ball out of play.

Mr Wright ran on, knelt over Kyle then called for Bernie to come and help. The caretaker brought a cold sponge and a towel. Soon Kyle was coming round and shaking his head, struggling to sit up.

'What's wrong with him?' Jimmy gasped.

'Looks like he hurt his head when he got flattened earlier on,' Jared said in a worried voice. 'That's how come he let in two easy goals.'

'They're carrying him off!' Leonie whispered. 'What are we gonna do now?'

Daisy turned to stare at their empty goalmouth. There were only a few minutes left of the match, but how could they hang on to their lead without a goalie?

Mr Wright came striding back on to the pitch with a grim look in his eye. 'Kyle's got concussion,' he announced. 'He's probably going to be OK, but we need a substitute goalkeeper.'

Daisy's heart missed a beat. Pity the poor person that Mr Wright chose!

'We want a safe pair of hands,' the sports teacher
insisted, scanning the players. 'Leonie, Jimmy and
Jared, we still need you up front in the role of strikers.'
His glance fell on Daisy.

'Oh no!' Daisy stammered. OK, so she'd practised
being in goal when she played in the park with Jimmy,
but no way could she do it for real! *Bam-bam!* Her heart
thumped against her ribs.

'Maybe, just maybe!' Mr Wright murmured.

'Not me!' she pleaded. 'Don't put me in goal, sir.
Please don't make me!'

Daisy crouched in the goalmouth.

Rain dribbled down the back of her neck. Her heart
had escaped from behind her ribs and was thumping
away in the region of her throat. *Buh-boom, buh-boom!*

'Swing lo-ow, sweet char-i-ot, comin' for to car-ry
me home!...'

They were into extra time and Woodbridge were
hanging on to their lead.

Captain Bell pounced on a loose ball and sped into
the Woodbridge half. Ponytail Kid was with him.

'Offside!' Nathan roared when Bell flicked the ball
to his sidekick.

The ref ignored the shout.

Daisy could see the boy's hair swinging behind him,
almost smell the mud on his boots when Leonie came

28

in from the side with a desperate tackle. Ponytail Kid went down with a blood-chilling yell, sprang up and claimed he'd been fouled.

The referee gave a penalty.

'Oh no!' Winona sighed, hiding her face behind her hands.

The crowd went deadly quiet.

The worst had happened. Only Daisy Disaster Morelli stood between the Marshway captain and a sudden-death-shoot-out for the Junior Inter Schools Cup!

'She'll never do it,' Bernie King groaned. 'Not Daisy Morelli!'

Mrs Waymann and Miss Ambler closed their eyes, afraid to look. After all, Daisy was not the substitute goalie *they* would have chosen either.

Buh-boom! Daisy's heart hammered.

'Come on, my Daisy, you show them!' A deep voice broke the silence.

Daisy looked up and saw her dad. He'd escaped from Pizza Palazzo for a few precious minutes to come and support the school team. He'd left Angie in charge and brought along baby Mia.

'We know you can save this ball!' Gianni called. 'We is all counting for you!'

'*On* me!' she muttered to herself. 'Counting *on* me!'

The grass had turned to mud under her feet, her

hands were slippery from the rain, Ponytail Kid was lining up to take the penalty.

He stared Daisy in the eye. She stared back.

Wham! He ran and kicked.

Whizz! She shot to one side, leaped through the air, arms outstretched. Her fingertips touched the ball, she curled her fingers, caught it to her and rolled to the ground.

'Yeah!' the Woodbridge fans yelled. 'Cool! Fantastic, Daisy! What a brilliant save!'

Four

It was the best moment of Daisy's life so far.

'Swi-ing low, sweet char-iot!' the Woodbridge fans sang as the ref blew the final whistle.

She grinned from ear to ear. Jimmy thumped her on the back and swore she was the best goalie in the country – no, in the whole world! Leonie did three forward-rolls then sprang up to swing from the crossbar. Jared pumped the air. They were the champions!

'The ref should never have given that penalty,' Nathan observed from the touchline. 'The Marshway player was well offside.'

'Wow, Nathan!' Winona sighed, sidling up to him and batting her long eyelashes. 'You know so much about the rules!'

'Daisy! My Daisy!' Gianni Morelli cried, running on to the pitch with Baby Mia.

'Gerroff, Dad!' Daisy squirmed as he tried to hug her. She ducked and did a lap of honour round the pitch with Jimmy and the others instead.

Yeah, the best moment. Covered from head to toe in mud, lungs bursting, legs aching, with rain dribbling down the back of her neck, Daisy couldn't believe that life got any better than this.

'And now for the presentation of the Helston Junior Inter-Schools Cup!' Mrs Waymann announced from underneath her purple umbrella.

Bernie King stood at her side holding a giant silver trophy. Fat Lennox growled at anyone who came near it.

The team from Marshway stood in line to receive the runners-up award. Their lanky captain looked crestfallen, while Ponytail Kid hung his head in shame.

'We are very lucky to have someone special here today to present the awards,' Mrs Waymann told the crowd.

Daisy stared eagerly at the bunch of grown-ups huddled around the Headteacher. *Someone special...*

'Who could it be?' Leonie muttered.

For a second Daisy dreamed it was a player from the Steelers' first team, or their famous coach. 'Kevin Crowe?' she whispered hopefully.

...And now the moment we've all been waiting for – Woodbridge Road Juniors line up to receive the Cup.

They take the long walk up the famous stairway, led by their magnificent captain, Jared Ikram, followed by hero of the moment, Daisy Morelli, whose miraculous save in the dying minutes of the game gave Woodbridge this fabulous trophy.

The team shakes hands with the Queen and the Duke of Edinburgh, and now Ikram leans forward for a word with Kevin Crowe, ex-England goalkeeper and coach of Premiership leaders, Steelers. Crowe turns to Morelli and congratulates her before he hands over the Cup. Now Ikram and Morelli lift it between them and the huge crowd goes wild!

'Our special guest is at the top of his profession. He rubs shoulders with some of the best known faces in the Premiership,' Mrs Waymann went on proudly.

'Or Robbie Exley!' Daisy breathed the name of the Steelers' star player to Leonie.

'And here he is to present the Cup – top professional referee, my husband, Michael Waymann!'

'Dream on, Daisy!' Leonie hissed, as Daisy's hopes burst like a pricked balloon.

Mousy Mr Waymann stood at the Headteacher's side. He had neat grey hair and a dark moustache, and was dressed in a navy blue padded jacket with a checked scarf.

'Since when was Witchy Waymann's husband a football referee?' Jimmy muttered.

'Who cares?' Jared answered, watching the Marshway players go up to shake hands with the visitor. 'We won, didn't we?'

And so they trotted up with heads held high, urged on by Mr Wright and cheered by the crowd.

'Well played,' Mr Waymann told Jared and Leonie, Jimmy, Daisy and the rest.

Bernie King held the Cup between his chunky hands. Lennox looked up and growled.

'We've seen some stars of the future here today,' Mr Waymann said, too softly for anyone except those closest to him to hear. 'Believe me – it's in the schools and in the local parks where the Robbie Exleys of tomorrow begin their brilliant careers!'

'Fat Lennox nearly bit my hand off!' Jared told Kyle. 'Honest, you should've seen him!'

Kyle had been sitting in Casualty with his dad when Mr Waymann had handed over the Cup. He'd missed the moment when the bulldog had bared his teeth and slavered.

'Ugly!' Jimmy said. 'The stupid dog must of thought the Cup was his!'

'Must *have*!' Winona corrected with a loud tut.

'Anyway, we won!' Leonie reminded them. It was Tuesday lunchtime, the day after the Cup Final, and the whole school was high on success.

Mrs Waymann had gone on about it during assembly, saying what it meant to Woodbridge Road Juniors to have the Junior Inter-Schools Cup for a whole year. She'd praised Mr Wright and the players, and said she wouldn't single anybody out for special mention, except to say that Kyle was home from hospital and back in school, and that he'd been a very brave boy to try and carry on as he did.

Mr Wright had gone around school with the biggest grin, and Miss Ambler had handed out mini Mars Bars to everyone in the team.

'Make the most of it,' Nathan had warned them, emerging from the library with a pile of books. 'We've got to finish our history assignment this afternoon, remember.'

But even this couldn't dampen Daisy's mood. Nor could Bernie King stomping down the corridor and giving her the evil eye.

'You might think you're king of the castle right now,' he muttered.

'I don't!' Daisy retorted. She was being honest. 'We were *all* brilliant, every single one of us!'

'But, believe me, it won't last,' the caretaker warned, striding on.

'What did you do to get up his nose this time?' Kyle wanted to know.

'Zilch! Zero! Nothing!' Daisy protested. *As usual!*

'She called Lennox a fat, slobbering idiot behind his back!' Leonie grinned, remembering the moment when Bernie had been forced to let go of the Cup and tug his dog off the playing field.

Daisy shrugged. 'Well, it's the truth.'

'Has anybody seen this?' Nathan asked, changing the subject and handing a brightly coloured leaflet to Leonie. 'I just spotted it on the librarian's desk.'

'Sorry, can't do it. I'll be in Spain,' Leonie sighed, reading the leaflet then handing it to Jared, who said his cousins were coming to stay, worse luck.

'What is it?' Jimmy snatched the paper and slowly read the front cover. 'Soccer School Special! Get your L...E...A to spo – spon...'

'Hey, give it here!' Daisy grabbed it from him. ' "Get your LEA to sponsor you!" she gabbled. ' "Join the Kevin Crowe Academy for a half-term training course." What's an LEA?'

'Local Education Authority,' Nathan told them patiently. 'It means you get someone in an office in town to pay you to play soccer.'

'Wow!' Jimmy's eyes were wide. 'Cool, or what!'

'Cool!' Daisy agreed. She read the inside of the leaflet. 'It's at the Steelers' training ground,' she explained. 'The course runs from Monday to Friday of half-term.'

'That's next week,' Winona pointed out. 'You're probably too late to put your name down.'

'You mean, we get to train at Highfield?' Jimmy gasped, ignoring Winona.

'If there's still time, and if there are any places left,' Nathan pointed out. He took his pet spider out of his schoolbag and opened the screw-top jar. 'Hi, Legs,' he said chattily, giving the spider's back a quick stroke.

Winona cringed and moved away.

'Highfield!' Jimmy breathed.

'You wanna do it?' Daisy asked Jimmy. Never mind what Nathan and Winona were saying, the idea of joining the Kevin Crowe Academy seemed pretty cool.

He nodded.

Daisy looked at him. He had that soccer-mad gleam in his eye. 'Me too!' she said. 'C'mon, let's go and ask Mr Wright!'

'No chance, I'm afraid,' the sports teacher said.

A herd of Year Twos stampeded into the gym, past Daisy and Jimmy. They smelled of stale trainers and sweaty, crumpled T-shirts.

'But sir!' Daisy protested. 'It says we can go for free and get the LEA to pay!'

Jimmy looked up at Mr Wright, his eyes round with excitement, his sticky-up hair standing out like a whole headful of exclamation marks.

'It's the first I've heard of it,' the teacher said.

So Daisy showed him Nathan's leaflet. 'See!' she

insisted. 'We get to go to the Steelers' training ground and tread on the grass that Robbie Exley's played on!'

'Yes, but have you filled in a form? Have you got a place on the course?' Mr Wright looked as if he'd like to help – after all, he was as soccer mad as the kids he taught – but he felt he had to point out the problems.

'You have to sign it, sir,' Daisy told him, 'then the school sends it off to an office in town and they say yes, and then it goes to Highfield…'

'Stop, stop!' Mr Wright handed back the form and headed off to control his Year Twos, who were climbing the wallbars and fighting over gym mats. 'Sorry kids, I think you're too late.'

Bump! Jimmy and Daisy's hearts plummeted.

'B-but, sir!' Daisy bleated, the teacher's harsh words echoing in her ears.

Five

'Don't be scared,' Nathan told Winona. He'd let Legs out of his jar and the spider was crawling across his *Meet the Normans!* book.

Winona sat next to him, her teeth clenched, her mouth stretched in a weird fake smile.

'I suppose Legs is quite cute!' Winona admitted in a squeaky voice.

Nathan's spider crawled up his pencil and perched on the rubber at the end.

Leonie overheard. 'You hate creepy crawlies!' she reminded Winona.

'Jared, don't talk when you're supposed to be reading!' Miss Ambler shrieked.

Miss Ambler was at the front of the class, telling Daisy and Jimmy off for being late. 'You know you have a history assignment to finish this afternoon, so what were you doing in the gym when you should have been here preparing?'

Blah-blah-blah! Daisy puffed out her cheeks and stared at the ceiling. It had been just their luck for Bernie King to come along and find them hanging round outside the gym after their talk with Mr Wright.

'Might have known!' the caretaker had growled, when he spotted them. 'Daisy Morelli and her little friend! You've no business being out of class, up to no good...'

'We were asking Mr Wright something important!' Daisy protested.

But Bernie collared them and marched them along to Miss Ambler. 'I found them skiving outside the gym,' he grunted. 'They spouted some nonsense about signing up for the Kevin Crowe soccer school during half-term.'

Daisy and Jimmy were landed at Rambler Ambler's desk like two slippery fish that Bernie had just caught. They had to listen to the caretaker's version of events.

'They'll be lucky,' Bernie scoffed. 'My nephew, William, plays for Steelers Juniors, and he says the course was full weeks ago!'

'No need for him to sound so pleased about it!' Daisy had muttered to Jimmy, who hadn't said a word through the whole thing. But his round eyes were narrowed into a frown, and his sticky-up hair seemed flatter.

'Jimmy, I'm disappointed in you,' Miss Ambler said now. 'You mustn't let Daisy lead you into trouble!'

('That was so not fair!' Daisy told Herbie later that evening. 'How come I always get the blame?')

'Daisy, isn't it possible that just for one day you could manage to do what you're supposed to?' Rambler Ambler moaned on.

('It was me who saved that penalty, remember!' Daisy grumbled to her stuffed hamster friend. 'You'd think they'd give me a break!')

When did William the Conqueror invade England?

Was it:

a) 1206

b) 1066

c) 1006

Daisy's pen hovered over the paper. *Dip-dip-dip, my blue ship ...* She ticked 1206 and went on to the next question.

Who was King of England at the time? Was it:

a) Henry

b) Harold

c) Hereward

Daisy's eyes glazed over. She heard the clash of spears on shields, the cries of men as they fell wounded on the ground.

'Find me a new horse!' the king cried, whirling round to face his brave ally, the Duke of Morelli. An arrow had pierced the side of the king's faithful white stallion, who lay dead on the ground beside him. 'The French outnumber us by ten to one. We must fight to the death to save England from the invader!'

Duke Morelli leaped from her own horse, then grabbed

the reins of a riderless mount. Her chain-mail armour hung

44

*heavy from her shoulders, her helmet cut into her forehead,
and she felt blood from the slash of an enemy sword run
down her cheek. 'I will stay by your side until death, my
liege!'*

*'We owe you our life!' The king bowed his head, then
galloped to the front of his tiny army. 'For England!' he
cried.*

*'For the King!' Morelli echoed, galloping alongside,
ignoring the flock of French arrows that met her.*

*'Morelli the Braveheart!' the king yelled above the clash
of swords. 'Your name will live forever in the history of this
great land!'*

"Hereward", Daisy wrote.

'It was King Harold!' Winona scoffed after the
assignment was finished. 'Everyone knows that!'

'Spiders! Creepy crawlies! Worms!' Daisy muttered
crossly, thinking of the things that Winona hated the
most.

'Actually, I like spiders now!' Ms Scaredy claimed,
giving Nathan a sickly smile. 'I think Legs is cute!'

'Watch out, Nathan: Winona fancies you!' Jared
warned.

As the whole class went 'Wooo-oooo!', Nathan took
off his glasses and wiped them with his hanky.

'Settle down!' Ambler sighed. 'Get on with your
private reading while I mark this work!'

'Listen!' Leonie insisted. The final bell had gone, and
only Jimmy, Daisy, Winona and Nathan were left in
the classroom. 'Do you and Jimmy still want to go to
this soccer school?'

'Yeah!' Jimmy and Daisy chirped.

'Are you coming, Nathan?' Winona had packed her
schoolbag and was hovering by the door, wearing her
sickly smile.

'Erm – er – no, I've got stuff to do,' Nathan
mumbled, hiding behind Leonie.

'Oh, for heaven's sake!' Winona tutted. She tossed
her curls and walked off.

'Phew!' Nathan sighed.

'As I was saying,' Leonie went on, gathering them
all into a huddle. Her brown eyes were bright and
sparkly as she leaned forward into the middle of the
group and began to whisper. 'If you want to get on to
the course, this is what you have to do…'

Six

The walk past the secretary's office, down the head teacher's corridor was the longest that Daisy and Jimmy had ever taken.

'You must be joking!' Daisy had gasped when Leonie had explained her plan.

'G-go and see Waymann?' Jimmy echoed. 'In her room? Right now?'

'Yes!' Leonie insisted. 'Listen. You know who Waymann's married to, don't you?'

'*Mister* Waymann,' Jimmy answered with a puzzled frown.

'Yes, but who *is* Mr Waymann? I mean, what does

he *do*?'

'He's a football referee,' Daisy chipped in.

'So!' Leonie waited for them to catch up.

Daisy and Jimmy pulled faces and shrugged.

'So he knows all the top players,' Nathan realised. 'He's probably best mates with Kevin Crowe.'

'Right!' Leonie's eyes gleamed. 'So you go to Waymann with your form and ask *her* to ask *him* to ask *Kevin* to give you both a place on the course!'

'Cool!' Daisy gasped, when she'd worked it out. Then, 'Hang on, did you say "go to Waymann"?'

Nathan too had spotted a problem. 'But what about the LEA?' he asked. 'They have to say yes as well.'

'That's where Waymann comes in.' Leonie had worked it all out. 'Daisy, you tell her it'll be really, really good for Woodbridge Road Juniors if we send our two star players to the course. Our school will be dead special – we'll have won the Cup *and* have two kids at the Academy!'

'Cool!' Nathan agreed. 'Then Waymann picks up the phone and speaks to the boss of the LEA. She's probably best mates with him. He says, sure, send Daisy and Jimmy along. We'll be glad to pay!'

'But we have to go and see her!' Daisy had got stuck on this bit of the plan. 'I mean, like, actually go and knock on her door!'

'Now!' Leonie insisted.

And she and Nathan had grabbed Jimmy and Daisy and dragged them to the main entrance hall.

And now they were walking down the dreaded corridor together, like two criminals going in front of the judge.

'I sentence you to ten years in prison, with hard labour.'

Daisy shuffled her feet in the dock. Her leg-irons clanked. Beside her, Jimmy hung his head and trembled. 'But what did we do?' she cried.

'Don't ask stupid questions. It's ten years' hard labour. Take them to the cells!'

Daisy and Jimmy swallowed hard and forced themselves to carry on walking. Past the big, framed photos of the school netball teams, past the glass-fronted cupboard containing the gleaming Inter-Schools Cup…

'We must be mad!' Daisy croaked. Never in her wildest dreams had she ever imagined walking down this corridor of her own free will.

OK, so there were times in any kid's life when you *had to* see the Head.

Like, for instance, when you accidentally kicked a football through Bernie King's window and he rushed out and caught you. Or when you'd been sent by Miss Ambler to fish frogspawn out of the school pond, but you let go of the plastic container and had to lie flat on your belly and reach out to get it back, but it sank, and you leaned too far and fell in…

But to be marching towards that tall, pale blue door, seeing that 'Please Knock' sign and touching that knob without being forced – well…

'We must be nuts!' Daisy said again.

'Let's turn back!' Jimmy hissed.

Look, the knob was turning without them touching it. The door was opening!

'Huh!' Bernie King squinted down at them. He rattled his bunch of keys as he came out of the Head's office.

'*Jailer, take them to the cells!*'

'*With pleasure, Judge!*'

'*Give them their prison clothes and feed them nothing but cabbage soup and stale bread. Make sure they work until their hands are covered in blisters!*'

The jailer jangled his keys. His short hair bristled like a stiff brush, his big hands grabbed the prisoners by the scruff of the neck. 'Leave it to me, Your Worship. I'll see that they suffer!'

'What are you two up to?' Bernie King asked them. 'No good, I bet!'

Ha-ha! Daisy screwed up her mouth. She glimpsed Mrs Waymann inside her room, sitting at her giant desk, and almost turned and scarpered.

'Who's there?' the Head barked.

Too late!

'Go on, get in if you're going.' Bernie shunted Daisy and Jimmy through the door and closed it behind them.

Yes, up to no good, he muttered to himself. With Daisy Morelli it was always light the blue touch paper and stand well back while the fireworks went off!

Well, will she fix it? Herbie asked.

Daisy had shot out of the Headteacher's room

with Jimmy as if there was a fire in the building.

'See you tomorrow!' she'd yelled at her friend, as she legged it out of the main front door, across the playground and down Woodbridge Road. She made it home in five minutes flat.

'Why are you out of breath?' her mum asked, rummaging in a drawer to find two matching socks for Mia. 'Who are you running away from?'

'Lah-lah-lah lu-la-lah!' Her dad had been singing as he bashed pizza dough into flat discs in the kitchen of Pizza Palazzo. 'Boom-boom-boom bu-ba-boom!'

Daisy had dashed upstairs and flopped down on her bed with Herbie.

'It was so scary!' she gasped. 'There's this ginormous desk with a phone and papers piled up everywhere. Waymann's got one of those swivel chairs that squeaks, with a flowery cushion on it.'

I know, I've seen it loads of times, Herbie reminded her. The Head's room was where he usually ended up when Miss Ambler confiscated him from Daisy.

('It's so not fair!' Daisy would fume. 'Ambler never con-fix-ates Legs!')

But did she fix for you to go to the course?

'We don't know yet.' Staring up at the ceiling with her hands behind her head, Daisy went through it with Herbie second by second.

There was Mrs Waymann smelling of roses, tapping

her fingernails on her ginormous desk. There was Jimmy standing next to Daisy, shaking all over, his knobbly knees knocking together. And Daisy herself going all croaky and trying to explain how great it would be for Woodbridge if she and Jimmy were sent to the soccer school.

Waymann: Tell me, Daisy, how exactly would it benefit the school if you went to Highfield?

Daisy: (with a croaky voice and struggling to remember what Leonie had told her to say) It just would, Miss.

Waymann: (glaring) My name is *Mrs* Waymann.

Daisy: Yes, miss. Sorry, miss. Er, Mrs Waymann.

Waymann: (tap-tap with her fingernails) Maybe it wouldn't be a bad thing for Woodbridge after all.

Daisy: (eagerly) Yes, miss. I mean, no, Mrs Waymann! It would show we were mega at sport. Lots of kids would want to come here!

Waymann: (looking sharply at Daisy) But would you be able to behave yourself for a whole week?

Daisy: I'd be really good, I promise. And we could get it in the newspaper. They could send a photographer and put us in the paper standing next to Kevin Crowe. It'd be cool, miss!

Waymann: (staring long and hard at a spot on the wall above Daisy's head) …I'll think about it.

She'll think about it? Herbie quizzed.

'Yeah, she'll probably ring the office in town before she goes home,' Daisy said, trying to sound more confident than she felt. 'Then she'll ask Mr Waymann to talk to his mate, Kevin Crowe.'

In your dreams! Herbie muttered quietly.

Daisy picked him up and stuffed him under her pillow. Honestly, sometimes he could be a pain.

'Daisy!' her mum's voice called up the stairs. 'There's someone to see you.'

Daisy sat up. It was probably Jimmy, here to talk over how it had gone in Waymann's office. 'Who is it?' she yelled back.

'It's Winona!' her mum said. 'Shall I send her up?'

This was mega hard to believe.

Curly-wurly Winona Jones was sitting cross-legged on Daisy's bed for a girly talk!

'I mean, what do you do if you fancy someone?' Winona sighed.

Daisy's mouth fell open. She was so not the person to ask! 'Dunno.'

'Oh come on, Daisy, you must know. Do you make it dead obvious, or do you play hard to get?'

'Don't ask me.' Daisy covered Herbie's ears so he didn't hear any of this.

Winona twiddled one of her curls. 'Only, the trouble with Nathan is that he doesn't seem – well – that interested in girls.'

'Nathan Moss?' Daisy swallowed hard and tried to keep her jaws clamped.

'Yes, don't look so surprised. You must have realised I fancied him. I've even tried to be nice to Legs!'

Daisy had to sit down. 'Nathan Moss!' she echoed feebly. Geeky Nathan with the mad hair and weird hobbies.

'He's so clever!' Winona sighed, taking off one of her patent leather shoes and rubbing off a tiny speck of dirt with the corner of Daisy's duvet. 'He just knows everything!'

That night, and at breakfast next morning, Daisy kept her fingers crossed. Today she would find out if Waymann had worked her witchy magic and got her and Jimmy a place at the Academy.

'Daisy, what are you doing? Leave Mia alone,' her mum said as she cleared the table.

'I'm teaching her to cross her fingers,' Daisy explained. 'See, Mia, if you want something so much it gives you a pain in your gut…'

'Daisy!' Angie Morelli warned.

'Sorry…a pain in your *stomach*, well, crossing your fingers can help because it's supposed to bring good luck.'

'Don't twist the baby's hands like that, she doesn't like it.'

'Goo-groo-gug,' Mia gurgled.

'Yes, she does. Look!' Daisy grinned and gurgled back at her baby sister. 'Cross your fingers for me, Mia. Jimmy and me are on our way to Highfield!'

'Wipe your face, wash the marmalade off your hands and don't dribble on your clean shirt,' her mum ordered.

'"Good luck, Daisy!"' Daisy mimed to Mia, racing to the sink and showing her hands and face a damp cloth.

'Goo-guck!' Mia said.

Angie and Daisy stopped dead.

'Did you hear that?' Angie gasped.

'Goo-guck, goo-guck-goo-guck!'

'She spoke!' Daisy's mum stammered. 'Daisy, go fetch your dad. Bring him here. Mia just said her very first words!'

On Wednesday morning, Kyle and Jared, Maya and Leonie, Winona and Nathan piled into the classroom as usual.

How can they act like everything's normal? Daisy wondered.

'Settle down, everyone!' Miss Ambler shouted. She was wearing her straggly brown hair back in a pony tail for a change, and had on a new pair of flat white shoes.

'It's 'cos she fancies Mr Wright!' Leonie giggled.

'Daisy, be quiet!' the teacher yelled.

Don't worry! Daisy said to herself. *Today is the big day. Wednesday. This time next week, we'll be kicking a ball around Highfield. Jimmy and me - we'll be superstars!*

'Daisy, pay attention,' Ambler said. '...Daisy, were you listening?...Daisy, I won't tell you again!'

They were halfway through the morning, and still there was no word from Waymann.

Daisy's fingers ached from being crossed. A frown had settled on to her face.

'What's up?' Jimmy asked.

'Nothing. OK, I'm dead nervous. What about you?'

Jimmy nodded. 'I don't think Waymann can of fixed it.'

'*Have* fixed it.' Winona corrected. 'Nathan, do you

like my drawing of King *Harold* being shot in the eye by an arrow?' She leaned across Daisy's desk. 'Miss Ambler is going to put it up on the wall!'

There was a sharp rap on the door and Bernie King walked in. 'I've come from the Head's office,' he told Miss Ambler. 'She wants a word with Jimmy Black and Daisy Morelli.'

Daisy grabbed the edge of her desk and flipped Winona's artwork on to the floor. This was it; the moment they'd been waiting for!

'Hey!' Winona whined, holding up the trampled drawing of the dead king.

Knock-knock! on the Head's blue door.

'Enter!' Mrs Waymann said. 'Ah, Jimmy and Daisy, come in! Would you like the good news first, or the bad?'

Daisy and Jimmy quaked in their shoes. This was definitely it!

'The g-good news!' Daisy croaked.

'Very well,' the Head said, peering over the top rim of her glasses. 'I've spoken to the LEA and they're prepared to sponsor you.'

Jimmy blinked and glanced at Daisy.

'They've said yes!' Daisy whispered out of the corner of her mouth. The smell of Mrs Waymann's perfume, wafting across the desk, was making her feel dizzy.

'Wicked!' Jimmy whispered back.

'But!' Waymann went on, tapping the desk with her fingernails. 'There is a snag.'

Daisy's head began to swim. The picture on the wall behind Mrs Waymann of the Woodbridge Road Junior Champion Girls' netball team, 1997-8, went fuzzy.

'When Michael rang the Academy and spoke to Kevin Crowe's secretary, he found that there were no places left on the course.'

Bummer! Big-big problem! Daisy sagged and hung her head.

'But!' Waymann said again, making them hang on to her every word. 'Michael asked to speak to Kevin in person, and when the big man himself came to the phone he agreed with my husband that they could manage to squeeze one more student on to the course.'

Daisy drew a sharp breath. Jimmy blinked again and threw her a worried look. 'It means that only one of us can go!' she hissed.

'That's the bad news,' Waymann told them, fixing them with her pitiless stare. 'We have to decide: is it going to be you, Jimmy Black, or you, Daisy Morelli?'

Seven

Daisy or Jimmy? Jimmy or Daisy?

They walked back into the classroom in a daze.

'So?' Leonie was the first to ask.

All eyes were fixed on them. Even Miss Ambler pressed the Pause button on the boring Bayeux Tapestry video and waited for their answer.

'It's either him or me,' Daisy mumbled.

'Who will stay and who will go?' The smiley presenter with the gelled hair and cheeky grin stared at the camera. The bright studio lights blinded Jimmy and Daisy, so that all they could see was a haze of cameras, and a sea of blurred

faces beyond. 'Will it be the talented guy with the wicked left foot and the shy smile? Or will it be the funky girl with the fastest body swerve in soccer? Audience, it's your chance to vote, so press your key-pads now!'

'Tough!' everyone said. 'How are they gonna choose?'

Quickly Ambler pressed the Play button and, without answering, Jimmy and Daisy sank into their seats.

At playtime, the whole school was talking about it. Would it be Jimmy or Daisy? The Year Twos wanted it to be Daisy, the Year Threes came out for late play and said it should be Jimmy. They went round in gangs chanting their favourite's name.

'Jimmy-Jimmy-Jimmy!'

'Dai-sy! Dai-sy!'

Daisy's nerves were strung out like stretched elastic. Waymann had said that she would talk to Mr Wright about who should be allowed to go, then let them know. But part of Daisy hoped that Jimmy would walk up to her and say, 'It's OK, Daisy, I don't care about it — you go!'

And, yes, there was even a teensy weensy corner of her brain that said, *Tell him you'll back down so he can go!*

But that didn't last long before she was back to crossing her fingers and praying that the games teacher would choose her.

'It's so not fair!' she muttered to Herbie behind the locked door of the girls' toilets. She just needed two minutes by herself. 'It's Jimmy against me, and he's my best mate!'

Hey, who ever said life was fair? the hamster replied.

So Daisy calmed down and the morning dragged on. She saw Jimmy, quieter than ever, pretending to work on his maths sheet. Leonie and Nathan had a race to finish first, then the door opened and Mr Wright came in to talk to Miss Ambler.

'Hello, Jon – er – Mr Wright!' Their teacher stood up and pushed a straggle of hair behind her ear. She was blushing and dithering as the two teachers put their heads together and mumbled.

'Soccer school...Jimmy...' Daisy overheard. *Huh!* She sighed and her heart sank.

'...Daisy!' Mr Wright went on.

Wow! Daisy crossed her fingers again, and everything else she could cross, plus bits she couldn't.

'Daisy...disaster...' Rambler Ambler muttered.

Oh no! Daisy's hopes were dashed again.

'Jimmy...too shy?' Mr Wright wondered.

Yes! Cool! Choose me! Daisy prayed.

'Wow, this is interesting!' Nathan whispered, looking up from his maths sheet. 'It's like two gladiators in Ancient Rome. The emperor has to save one, and the other gets thrown to the lions, raa-aagh!'

'Thanks, Nathan!' Daisy groaned.

Audience, press your key-pads!

Daisy closed her eyes. She felt sick. She mustn't miss the chance to train at Highfield, to tread the turf, to kick a ball where Saint Robbie had kicked! On the other hand, poor Jimmy! He wanted this just as much as her. He had Robbie Exley posters all over his room, even on the ceiling. If they didn't choose him, he'd probably die of a broken heart.

Daisy gave Jimmy a quick, sad smile and he gave her one back.

'Daisy?…Jimmy?…we must make a decision,' Mr Wright told dithery Miss Ambler.

Then…like a bolt of lightning from the blue sky… like a referee of the vast heavens spreading her wings and taking out a red card…like a Roman emperor in the lions' arena…Mrs Waymann swept into the room!

Daisy and Jimmy took deep breaths.

'Wonderful news!' the head teacher announced. 'I've just had a phone call from Kevin Crowe. There's been a late cancellation. Daisy and Jimmy have *both* got a place at the soccer school!'

Eight

'Swi-ing low, sweet char-i-ot…!' Daisy sang as she washed dishes.

'Mum, shall I empty the bins for you? Does Mia's nappy need changing? Sit down, let me make you a cup of tea!'

Angie Morelli sat with her feet up in front of the telly. 'What happened to my grumpy, messy daughter?' she asked. 'Who brought this little angel in her place?'

'Ha-ha!' Daisy brought tea and her mum's favourite ginger biscuits. She'd been in a mega mood for two days now, ever since Waymann had made her announcement. In fact, she'd been floating; her feet hadn't touched the ground.

Not even when Ambler told her she'd got all the questions except one wrong in her maths test, or when Winona cornered Daisy and whinged about Nathan.

'What's wrong with him?' Winona asked. 'I'm making it dead obvious that I fancy him, but he just talks about the latest bus ticket he's collected!'

'Try music,' Daisy suggested kindly. 'Nathan's mad keen on playing the trumpet.'

And she'd floated on with a smile, through the whole of Thursday and Friday, even ignoring Bernie King, who collared her outside his basement office.

'Jammy beggar!' he sneered, while wheezy fat Lennox prowled and sniffed. 'I heard what happened …another kid gave up his place at the last minute and they let you in.'

Daisy nodded and hummed 'Swing low' under her breath.

'Jammy!' Bernie said again. 'I only hope they know what they're letting themselves in for!'

And now school had closed for half-term, and everyone except Bernie had said good luck to Jimmy and Daisy.

'Lucky things!' Jared sighed, before going off for boring tea with his cousins.

'Enjoy!' Leonie told them. 'Think of me in sunny Spain!'

Mr Wright had given them high-fives and said it was the chance of a lifetime.

'Only two days to go,' Daisy reminded her mum now, settling down on the sofa with her.

'As if I needed telling.' Angie sipped her tea. She'd just put the baby to bed and was taking five minutes before she went to wait tables in the café.

'Saturday tomorrow,' Daisy said. 'Steelers play Malton United. Ashby City are level with us in the Premiership with only two matches to go before the end of the season, so we need to beat Malton.'

'Hmm.' Angie sat there with a glazed look.

'Mu-um…'

'What?'

Daisy knew she was pushing her luck. Her mum and dad weren't rich, there was never much money to spare. But this was special, so she blundered on. 'I saw some cool footie boots in the sports shop window. Jimmy and me just happened to be passing. They don't cost much, and my old ones are way too small. They really make my toes hurt…'

Saturday evening, and Daisy was staring down at a pair of shiny new boots! She wore them inside the house, in the Pizza Palazzo and in her bedroom.

'Aren't they cool?' she asked Herbie a hundred times. 'They're a copy of the ones Robbie wears!'

OK, so Steelers had lost one - nil to Malton United, but their rivals Ashby City had lost too, so it was still level at the top of the table. Everyone had agreed that the penalty should never have been given against Steelers defender, Marc Predoux. But her mum had said yes to new boots, and anyway, there was still one match left in the season – Steelers versus Ashby City – the big derby match. If Steelers won, the Premiership was theirs.

So Daisy hadn't hopped down from Cloud Nine, and she was only two nights and one day away from walking through the players' entrance on City Road.

'You hear what happened?' Gianni Morelli told his customers on Sunday as the pizzas sizzled. 'You see my Daisy here? She has been picked to go to soccer school! Believes me, I am the happiest man in Helston!'

One of his diners just happened to be Karl Andrews, a sports reporter on the *Helston Herald*. 'Sounds good,' Karl told Daisy's dad, tucking into a massive pizza margerita. 'I'll try to get down there and do an interview.'

'We're gonna be famous!' Daisy told Jimmy. 'We'll be in the newspaper – a picture and everything!'

Goal!

Morelli scores her second!

Zap, into the back of the net!

Wham! Zap! Whoosh!

In her dreams, Daisy went on scoring goals. She kicked the duvet off her bed and threw Herbie in the air. She hugged her pillow and ended up on the floor with a bump.

She woke up. It was still dark, but she slung on her football kit and new boots, then headed along the landing, *clunk-clunk*.

'Goo-guck, goo-guck!' Mia's muffled chant followed her downstairs.

In the sitting room Daisy decided to do press-ups until dawn.

It was only a few hours now before Daisy and Jimmy passed through that famous gate.

'Hi Marc, hi Robbie, hi Kevin!' They would greet their heroes like best mates, get lifts home in their Porsches, meet their glamorous girlfriends and go out clubbing together.

'Hey Daisy, you rock, y'know that!' Marc Predoux would praise her neat tackles and curving corner kicks.

Kevin Crowe would watch from the manager's dugout, not saying much, but noting Daisy's work rate and commitment to the game.

Twenty-one, twenty-two, twenty – ergh! Daisy flopped to the floor, her arms limp as two strands of cooked spaghetti. *Zzzz!* She was still there two hours later when her mum came in to open the curtains.

And in the end, it happened in a blur. Daisy gulped breakfast while Jimmy fidgeted by the door, dressed in his blue Steelers shirt, white shorts and blue socks.

'We're gonna be late!' he warned. 'It's our first day, we can't get there after the others!'

'No problem!' Daisy's dad declared, looking at his watch. 'I take you in my car!'

So Daisy and Jimmy made their grand entrance at Highfield in a white van with Pizza Palazzo written in giant red letters on the side. There was a picture of a scrummy pizza on the back doors and a big dent on the bonnet from when Daisy's dad had driven into a builder's skip.

Daisy and Jimmy scrambled out of the back of the van. Daisy's rucksack was stuffed with sandwiches and a cagoule in case it rained. Oh, and Herbie was zipped up safely inside the front pocket after he'd made it clear that he would never speak to Daisy again if she left him behind.

I mean it! he'd said, his one beady eye burning a hole in her.

'This is it!' Jimmy whispered, looking up at the back

of the giant main stand.

Daisy swallowed hard. 'This is it!' she echoed. *Me, Daisy Angelina Morelli, stepping out with my best mate, Jimmy Black, waving goodbye to my dad, standing under letters half a mile high that spell out the name of Steelers, the best football team in the entire world!*

'Wow!' Jimmy breathed.

The players' gate opened and Daisy and Jimmy walked in.

Nine

'Welcome to Highfield!' Gary Ford said.

Inside Daisy's chest, an invisible drummer beat a jerky rhythm against her ribs. Wow, was she nervous!

Gary Ford was Steelers' youth-team coach – he was even older than Daisy's dad and had played centre forward for Malton United way back in ancient history. He had a bald head and a bit of a beer belly, but he was still cool.

'You kids don't know how lucky you are!' Gary told the ten soccer hopefuls lined up in front of him on the training pitch. 'People would kill to get the chance you've been given, so make the most of it!'

Boom-boom, buh-boom, rat-a-tat, whoosh! The sun shone, the breeze blew, and green grass smooth as a snooker table spread out before Daisy and her drumming heart.

'We're going to start with fitness training,' Gary explained. 'I want you to ignore the groundsmen working on the goalmouths and jog around the outside of the pitch until you loosen up. OK, go!'

Rat-a-tat, rat-a-tat, bee-bop, boom! Daisy jogged ahead of Jimmy, behind a long-legged black kid about twice as tall as her. She found she had to sprint to keep up, past the groundsmen, down the far side of the pitch.

'Good, now I want you to put in short bursts of speed,' Gary told them when they'd jogged for five minutes.

Daisy's shoulders sagged. "Bursts of speed" didn't sound good.

'No slacking. Come on, get a move on, go!'

'I'm so not fit!' Daisy gasped.

Jimmy too had to bend double to catch his breath.

On the first morning at Highfield they'd done an hour and a half of fitness training, and so far they hadn't so much as seen a football, let alone a famous player or Kevin Crowe.

Darren, the kid with the long legs, breezed by. 'Got a problem?' he asked Jimmy and Daisy.

'Nope!' they yelped, standing upright and ignoring the pounding of their hearts.

'Work, work, work!' Gary Ford insisted. 'Any kid can kick a ball around a park, but in this game, at the top level fitness is what counts!'

Gasp-gasp! 'I'm never gonna make it!' Daisy groaned.

'Me neither!'

Gary had strolled to the touchline to fetch a net full of balls. When he came back, he was in a softer mood. 'Look,' he said. 'I know each one of you is the star of your own school team, and you must be wondering why I'm being so tough on you. But you're playing in the big time now. Kevin will only want to take a look at you later this week if he sees you're willing to put in the work. You have to give it one hundred and ten percent!'

As the youth-team coach talked, Daisy sneaked a look around. She saw half a dozen groundsmen rolling and prodding the turf, plus a couple of players in training kit standing at the edge of the pitch. Her heart skipped – could it be Marc Predoux, or even Robbie Exley?

Gary Ford spotted them too. 'Hey, Shane and William, come and say hi!'

The two players trotted towards the kids. Closer to, Daisy made out that they were about fifteen or sixteen years old – one lean and lanky with carroty red hair, the other shorter and stockier with fair, cropped stubble.

'Kids, this is Shane, and this is William. They're training with the club and play in the junior squad.'

'Wow!' Jimmy breathed. 'That could be us in a few years, Daisy!'

'Yeah, when the FA finally decides to let girls play,' she muttered back. Staring at William, she couldn't get rid of the idea that his face looked familiar.

'How's it going? Is Gary working your socks off?' Shane asked Jimmy, casually flicking a ball towards him.

Jimmy trapped the ball under his left foot then flipped it up on to his knee and kept it in the air.

'Neat!' Shane grinned, and pretty soon the two young club players were training with the school kids.

Then three more joined them. Footballs were whizzing across the pitch and arching through the air.

'This is so cool!' Daisy grinned at Jimmy, taking a pass from William and flicking it forward to her best mate.

'Jimmy Black, pass back to Daisy Morelli!' Gary shouted from the touchline.

'Hey, are you two from Woodbridge Road Juniors?' William asked, as Daisy received the ball and swerved past him.

'Yeah, how did you know?' She passed ahead to Darren Longlegs.

'My uncle happened to mention it.'

Daisy stopped. 'Your uncle?' Now it began to make sense. This was why she'd thought she knew William. Stocky build – stubbly head – yeah, now she got it. But, hey, it was bad news!

'Uncle Bernie,' William told her. 'Bernie King – he works at your school!'

'How rotten is that!' Daisy groaned, her mouth full of cheese and pickle sandwich.

It was midday. The soccer academy kids sat in the changing room eating their packed lunches.

'Rotten,' Jimmy agreed.

'It turns out Bernie's told William all about me,' Daisy sighed, opening up her sandwich and adding a layer of crisps to the cheese and pickle. 'It's so not fair – he said I'm always in trouble and my middle name's Disaster!'

'Yeah, but William didn't believe him, did he?' Jimmy asked.

Daisy shrugged. 'Dunno. He was grinning when he said it.'

'See.'

'Yeah, but...' Daisy trailed off, staring along the rows of empty hooks where players like Robbie and

Marc got changed. 'It gets worse,' she added gloomily.

Jimmy finished his carton of orange juice then pulled his socks up over his skinny knees. 'How come?'

'Bernie's actually gonna be here!'

'When? Where?' Jimmy glanced round, as if the school caretaker might be hiding under a bench.

Daisy shook her head in despair. She could see it now - with Bernie King spreading bad things about her all around Highfield, they would soon be calling her Daisy Disaster Morelli all over again.

'Come on, when? How come?' Jimmy insisted.

'Tomorrow. He's gonna be a groundsman,' Daisy sighed. 'William says Kevin Crowe rang Bernie up and asked him to help out!'

'This training ground needs a new drainage system!' Bernie declared. He was there at Highfield when Jimmy and Daisy arrived next morning, his loud voice booming down the corridor. 'You need to rip up the turf and start all over again!'

Daisy cringed and hid in a corner.

'Hug-hug-huh!' Fat Lennox sniffed her out.

'Gerroff!' Daisy whined. Nightmare! Bad-Breath Lennox was wheezing all over her.

'With the money this club earns, laying new drains is nothing!' Bernie went on and on. 'If I was head groundsman, I'd put it top of my list!'

'*Sniff-huh-slurp!*'

'Phwoah, fat Lennox, get lost!'

The bulldog seemed pleased to see her, unlike his master.

'Daisy Morelli, I might have known you'd be here causing trouble,' Bernie grumbled, stomping across to rescue his dog. He tugged at Lennox's thick, studded collar while Daisy made her escape.

'How come your uncle gets invited to be a groundsman?' she complained to William King when she spotted him heading for the changing room.

'They're one man short,' William answered. 'And Uncle Bernie used to work across town at the Ashby City ground when he was younger. He knows what the job involves.'

'Great!' she sniffed.

'Come on, Daisy, get a move on!' Gary Ford told her, striding round the corner into view. 'I want to see you out there on the pitch in two minutes flat!'

Once Daisy was out there training, she soon forgot about the grumpy caretaker and his smelly dog. She jogged and sprinted, swerved and turned, sure that she was getting fitter with every step she took.

'Nice one, Daisy!' Gary Ford yelled as she smoothly dribbled a ball for twenty metres towards the goalmouth. 'Come on, Jimmy, let's see what you can do.'

'Hm!' Bernie King grunted, resting on the machine that made the white lines. 'Let's see how long you can keep this pace up!'

Daisy ignored him, picked up her ball and sprinted away.

'Anyhow, Bernie King can't even keep his white lines straight,' Daisy muttered to Jimmy not long afterwards. 'See that one with the big wobble in it? That's his!'

'Sprint, stop, turn to the right, sprint again!' Gary ordered.

Ten kids ran their legs off.

'Jump, squat, jump, turn, sprint!'

'I'm worn out!' Daisy groaned when the coach gave them a ten-minute break. She flopped down on the grass and lay flat on her back.

Squeak-sqeak! Bernie pushed his white liner along the turf. 'Can't take it, eh?' he muttered to Daisy. 'I told our William they should never have let you on to the course.'

'OK, time to move!' Gary called. 'Jog four times round the pitch, then grab a ball. First one back to me gets a gold star!'

'Uh-uhhh!' Daisy's legs ached, her lungs felt like they would burst. *I don't want to be a soccer super star!* she decided. *I've changed my mind!*

'The girl's got no stamina!' Bernie King observed her slowing down. He spoke loud enough for Daisy to hear.

So she gritted her teeth and put on a spurt.

'Nice work, Daisy!' Gary told her when she got back to him ahead of all the rest. 'Michael Waymann said I should look out for you. He reckons you're a good little player.'

'M-me?' Daisy gasped.

'Yes. He's a mate of mine. I saw him earlier this morning, as a matter of fact.'

Daisy held her head high. *A good little player!* Bernie King could say what he liked – no way was he going to ruin her week in soccer heaven!

Ten

'Winona's here!' Daisy's mum called upstairs.

'Uhhh!' Daisy groaned. *Not again!*

Trip-trip-trip - Winona breezed daintily up the stairs and into Daisy's room.

Daisy lay flat on her back with Herbie squidged cosily on her stomach. Every muscle in her body ached.

'Hi!' Winona said. 'Do you fancy coming to Nathan's house with me?'

'No way!' Daisy sighed.

'Good, come on then!'

'I said no!'

Winona sniffed and pulled Daisy into a sitting position. Herbie slid sideways on to the floor.

Ouch! he squeaked.

'You have to come, Daisy. Oh, and by the way, you can play the recorder, can't you?'

Daisy flopped back on the bed. 'No.'

'Cool, 'cos I'll lend you one. I've got my violin. We're going to Nathan's to practise music.'

Daisy glowered sideways at Winona. How come Ms Perfect was so friendly all of a sudden? And how come she didn't ask Daisy how she'd got on at Highfield? 'I'm too tired,' she moaned.

And I'm trapped under Winona's pesky foot! Herbie pointed out. *Ouch! Ouch!*

'Nathan will be playing his trumpet. I said I'd be there at six,' Winona went on. She tugged Daisy off the bed, dusted her down and spruced her up.

Ten minutes later, though she groaned and sighed, Daisy was eeking and squeaking on Winona's recorder in Nathan's living room.

'There was spit coming out of the end and dribbling on to the carpet!' Daisy told Jimmy next morning as she fastened her boots in the Highfield changing room.

'Yuck!'

'Yeah, yuck. Nathan's brother came in and told us to

stop making a racket. He said Nathan's trumpet sounded like a cow in pain.'

'Poor you,' Jimmy sympathised.

'Winona only used the music as an excuse for going round to chat Nathan up. She wormed her way in there, with me tagging along like a spare part.'

'Huh.'

'Now she's telling everyone she's going out with Nathan.'

'Come on, Daisy, get a move on!' Jimmy was up and raring to go. He slipped past the ground staff hanging around in the corridor and out on to the pitch.

'Huh, late as usual.' Bernie King spotted Daisy.

'Give the poor kid a break,' another voice said.

Daisy glanced over her shoulder to see Mrs Waymann's husband hanging out with the groundsmen. He was dressed in a grey suit and carrying a briefcase. She smiled shyly at him then hurried on.

Outside, Gary Ford was already waiting for them with new exercises for their aching muscles.

Daisy was grunting and puffing her way down the pitch behind Darren Longlegs when she spotted another face she knew. It was a second man in a suit, strolling along the touchline with Mr Waymann.

'That's Kevin Crowe!' Jimmy hissed, sprinting

alongside and watching the Steelers manager shake hands with Michael Waymann and break away towards Gary Ford.

Daisy nodded and tried to put a spring into her step. *Impress – impress!* she told herself, pumping her arms like pistons to make herself run faster. Around here, Kevin Crowe was *God!*

After five minutes, Gary gathered the kids for a team talk and Kevin himself spoke.

'Great to see you here at the Academy!' he told them. 'You're the future of the sport – just remember that!'

Wow! Daisy's eyes were out on stalks. Kevin Crowe was smiling at them and saying nice things. He looked like he did on the telly – neat dark hair greying at the sides, tanned face, sharp suit.

'Hey, and how would you stars of the future like to meet the stars of today?' Kevin asked.

'Yeah!' they cried. 'Cool!'

And, before their very eyes, without fuss, out came the entire Steelers first team! They strolled in twos and threes, chatting and laughing, heading towards the kids from the soccer school.

'That's Marc Predoux!' Jimmy breathed, picking out the player's black hair plaited in tiny, neat rows and held back in a ponytail. 'And Hans Kohl and Pedro Martinez!'

'And Robbie!' Daisy sighed. She only had eyes for
him.

Robbie Exley!

Her hero's blond, corn-stubble hair shone in the sunlight. His handsome, square-jawed face was turned towards them.

Bazam! Soccerman took off from the ground, his blue cloak streaming behind him. With clenched fist, he rose to the top of the tower block and hovered in the air.

'Save me! Save me!' Daisy Darling cried, clinging to a narrow window ledge on the fiftieth floor.

Beside her, arch enemy Dastardly Don aimed his ray gun at Soccerman.

Zap! The legend kicked out with his right foot, blasting the gun from Don's hand. Wham! With his left boot, Soccerman landed a killer blow on the villain's jaw.

'Daisy!' Jimmy hissed.

'Huh?' Daisy came to with a start.

'That man with the camera wants you.'

'What man?' Back down to earth, she saw that the Steelers' first team had lined up on the pitch for an official photo session. A photographer had got them in two rows, with Kevin and Robbie in the middle.

'He's from the Helston Herald,' Jimmy said. 'He says he wants you in the picture!'

Daisy gasped as she recognised Karl Andrews – her dad's regular customer at the Pizza Palazzo.

'Hey!' he called to Daisy. 'Get over here quick!'

'C'mon!' Daisy told Jimmy. No way was she going to leave her best mate behind.

Together they sprinted across.

'Get in the photo!' Karl said, raising his camera to his eye. 'Go on, both of you, squeeze in!'

'Cool!' Jimmy breathed, plonking himself down in front of Kevin Crowe and putting on a cheesy grin.

'Somebody pinch me!' Daisy muttered. Robbie Exley had arranged her in front of him, dead in the middle of the team photograph.

'This will be in the *Herald* tomorrow morning,' Karl told them, aiming his camera. 'Kevin's set it up. It's a special piece on young talent at the Soccer Academy.'

'We'll be famous!' Jimmy sighed, his eyes gleaming.

Daisy grinned and grinned.

'OK, guys, look this way!' Karl said.

Click!

Daisy and Jimmy sitting cross-legged in front of Robbie Exley. Grinning like idiots.

Click! Click!

Eleven

Local Kids Hit the Heights was the top headline on the sports page of the *Helston Herald* next day. ***Are Daisy Morelli and Jimmy Black the Stars of Tomorrow?***

'Mum, watch out!' Daisy made a desperate grab for the newspaper spread out on the kitchen table.

Too late. Mia had splatted her baby breakfast all over the photo of Daisy and Jimmy.

'Ergh!' Daisy wiped it off with her hand, but the picture was ruined.

'Goo-guck!' Mia gurgled.

'Never mind, I'll get another,' her mum promised. 'In fact, I expect your dad's down at the paper shop right now, buying up their entire stock of *Helston Heralds*!'

Sure enough, Gianni Morelli staggered in with a pile of papers. 'One for your grandmother in Rome!' he announced proudly. 'One for my brother in Naples. One for your cousins in Rimini…!'

Daisy's mum laughed as she cleared away the breakfast mess. 'You're nearly halfway through the week, Daisy. How does it feel?'

'Mega!' she smiled, then made faces at her baby sister. 'Mum-mum-mum!' she mouthed. 'C'mon, Mia, say "Mum"!'

'Goo-guck!' Mia replied.

'I make a good, special pizza for Karl next time he comes!' Gianni promised. 'Lots of herbs and garlic, lots of cheese!'

Daisy grabbed her soccer kit from the drier and stuffed it into her bag. 'Did I tell you, Robbie wished me luck?' she asked her mum, hugging her shirt to her chest.

'Yep, about a hundred times!'

'Did I tell you, Herbie?' Daisy fished in her bag and dragged him out.

Herbie stared with his one eye but said nothing.

'OK, so I'm sorry – I left you in the bag overnight. I forgot about you. But I was dead excited about the team photo, and I'm sorry, sorry, sorry!'

Herbie sulked and stared.

'Go on, you'll be late!' Angie said, hustling Daisy out of the door. 'Hi, Jimmy! That's a good photo of you in the paper!'

Jimmy's grin said it all as he hovered by the door.

'Go!' Angie told Daisy.

Today was Day Three of Daisy heaven.

'This is a big year for Steelers!' Daisy's dad talked soccer with Jimmy on the way to Highfield. 'We have good chances of winning the Premiership and getting into Europe!'

'Yeah, we only have to beat City on Saturday,' Jimmy reminded him. 'We're joint top at the moment, with only this one match to go.'

'We'll make it!' Daisy said. On a morning like this,

with the sun glinting on the Steelers' stadium sign as
she and Jimmy stepped out of the van, what could
possibly stop them finishing top of the table?

'Race you to the changing rooms!' Jimmy cried,
darting through the players' gate.

'Race you on to the pitch!' Daisy challenged, when
she and Jimmy met up in the corridor after they'd got
changed.

Darren and a couple of other kids blocked Jimmy's
way, so she got out first.

'Hey, Daisy, nice picture of you in the paper today!'
Gary Ford greeted her. 'Listen, would you run back
and fetch a ref's whistle from my office? I forgot to
bring one.'

Eagerly Daisy trotted back into the building. With
luck she could spin this out and miss a few of the
warm-up exercises.

She jogged down the corridor, past the changing
rooms. Now, which was Gary's office? Not that one –
that was the mighty Kevin Crowe's room. And not this
gleaming, posh one with *Managing Director* written on
the door.

Daisy was slowing down, feeling lost, as she turned
a corner and faced a new corridor and a fresh set of
doors.

'...Don't let Kevin hear you say that!' a voice said from
the first room to her right.

A second person gave a short, sharp laugh. 'What d'you think I am – stupid?'

Daisy hesitated. The first voice sounded like Bernie King's, but she couldn't be sure.

'Don't even mention the words *Ashby City* around here!' the first man said.

Holding her breath, Daisy peered through the open door. There were desks with banks of computers, and two men with their backs to her. Yes, she was right – it was the dreaded Bernie, talking, as it turned out, to Michael Waymann. She bobbed back out of sight before they saw her.

'What is it that you do with all these computers?' Bernie asked, wandering up to a nearby desk.

'I keep a couple of Premiership websites up to date, and stuff like that,' Mr Waymann answered. 'As well as being a referee, I'm a computer programmer. Updating websites is part of the deal.'

'Hmm.' Bernie sounded interested. 'Do you go into the City ground as well?'

Outside the door, Daisy frowned. How was she going to get past without being seen? No way did she want Bernie pouncing on her and demanding to know what she was up to.

'Sometimes,' Michael Waymann admitted.

'Now that *is* interesting!' Bernie grunted.

'*Hugh-huh-huugh!*' Fat Lennox came wheezing around

the corner in search of his master. *'Grrrrgh!'* he said when he saw Daisy.

'Do these computers let you see the players' contracts?' Bernie went on. 'Do you know exactly how much Steelers pay Robbie Exley, say?'

Why did Bernie King want to know? Daisy was holding her breath and staring down at Lennox.

'Grrrrgh!'

'...*Very* interesting!' Bernie was saying. 'Wait here, Michael, while I fetch the dog and close the door ...'

'Bernie King is a spy!' Daisy announced.

'Don't be daft!' Jimmy said. He was worn out after another hard day's training. Now all he wanted was to veg out in front of the telly.

'He is!' Daisy had gone round to Jimmy's house to spill out her news. She'd carried it round all day and now she was bursting to let it out. 'Bernie King is a spy for Ashby City.'

The tune played for the end of *Neighbours* and Jimmy pressed the Off button. 'What kind of spy?' he asked.

'You know – a *spy* spy! Snooping round, selling secrets, working for the enemy!'

'How d'you know?' Jimmy stuffed his mouth full of prawn cocktail crisps, scrunched the packet and drop-kicked it into the bin.

'I heard him. He's getting Mr Waymann to be a computer hacker. They're hacking into Steelers' computers and selling information to Ashby City! They are, Jimmy, trust me!'

Her friend shrugged. '*When* did you hear?'

'This morning, when Gary sent me for the whistle.' She'd heard enough to be sure, even before Bernie had come to the door to grab Lennox and haul him inside and Daisy had made a quick dash round the corner, out of sight.

After that, Bernie had shut her out, but she'd still been able to hear the muffled words through the door, 'City…title race…Robbie….contract…'

'Yeah, you skiver, you took ages bringing that whistle,' Jimmy remembered.

'Listen, Jimmy, Bernie's plan is to steal Robbie Exley for Ashby City! They're gonna pay him shed-loads of money. Then, without our star player, we're gonna lose the Premiership!'

'You're nuts!' Jimmy said, switching the telly back on for *The Simpsons*.

Daisy planted herself in front of the screen. 'You've gotta believe me, Jimmy! Am I ever wrong about stuff like this?'

Jimmy screwed up his mouth and thought for a while. 'Yep. There was the time when you thought Leonie had dobbed you in for nicking her homework.

Then when you said Robbie had broken his leg in training, and he hadn't. And yesterday when you told me that Winona was going out with Nathan, and I just saw Nathan and he says he's not...'

'Yeah, yeah, yeah!' Daisy pushed these to one side. 'But I'm right this time, honest. Bernie's a spy!'

'But why?' Jimmy insisted. 'He's one of us. He's a Steelers fan!'

Daisy's eyes narrowed. She grabbed the TV control and dabbed the Off button. 'That's where you're wrong,' she whispered. 'Bernie pretended to be one of us so he could worm his way into being a part-time groundsman at Highfield, but really he's the enemy!'

'Prove it!' Jimmy said, fighting Daisy for the remote.

Daisy held on to it, and in the silence she played her trump card. 'I'll give you proof!' she declared. It was a fact that Jimmy wouldn't be able to deny. 'William told us Bernie King used to work for Ashby City, remember? So they trained him to steal secrets from the enemy. It's true, Jimmy – Bernie King is a low-down, rotten spy!'

Twelve

Daisy showed up at Winona's house overlooking the school playing fields when Winona was helping her mum with the ironing.

'Ironing?' Daisy gasped.

'Yes, I *like* ironing!' Winona insisted, coming out into the garden to hear Daisy's story.

'Bernie King…Mr Waymann…Steelers…Ashby City!' Daisy gabbled. If Jimmy wouldn't believe her, she'd soon find someone who would.

'How does Mr Waymann come into it?' Winona asked.

'Waymann only works part-time as a referee,' Daisy told Winona. 'The rest of the time he works with computers!'

'Oh no, not computers!' Winona threw up her hands in mock horror. 'Don't they put you in prison for that?'

'I'm serious,' Daisy insisted. 'He can get into the computer rooms at Highfield and at Low Moor, Ashby City's ground. I bet he knows secret passwords and everything!'

'But Jimmy thinks you're wrong,' Winona pointed out. 'And Jimmy even believed you when you said Miss Ambler was going out with Robbie Exley!'

'Yeah, well…' Daisy regretted the trick she'd played on poor Jimmy that time.

Winona flicked her hair, then decided to play along with Daisy for a while. 'Let me get this straight. Mr Waymann is a hacker. Bernie King is a spy. So what do you want *me* to do?'

'We've got to stop them!' Daisy cried.

'But how?' Little Miss Innocent frowned and pretended to think. 'Hey, I've got an idea!'

'What?' Daisy's heart leaped. At last someone believed her.

'We've got to go and see Nathan!' Winona decided with a determined glint in her eye. 'He's so clever, he's bound to know what to do!'

'No way!' Nathan said.

Daisy and Winona had climbed the hill to his house
overlooking City Road. They'd heard him practising the trumpet as they walked up the path and knocked at the door.

'Einstein, there's two gorgeous women at the door for you!' Nathan's older brother, Luke, had called.

The trumpet notes had whined to a halt and Nathan had appeared.

'Mr Waymann...Bernie King...007...James Bond!' Winona had gabbled out Daisy's story, with Luke still hanging round in the hallway.

'I never said anything about James Bond,' Daisy had muttered.

'OK, but Bernie King is a spy!' Winona had insisted. 'We want you, Nathan, to help uncover the secret plot against Steelers!'

And that was when he'd come out with his answer. 'No way!'

'Aah, Einstein, why not?' Luke teased. 'I fancy my little bro doing the James Bond, 007 stuff!'

'Don't call me Einstein, and butt out of this,' Nathan snapped back, running a hand through his mad, messy hair. Then he turned to Winona. 'Listen, I don't believe a word of what Daisy told you.'

'Hey, do you mind not talking about me as if I wasn't here!' Daisy cut in. She was one hundred percent sure of what she was telling them. 'Listen, Nathan, I thought you were a Steelers fan!'

Nathan shrugged and turned away. 'I have to practise my trumpet,' was all he said.

'So anyway, who cares!' Daisy told Herbie as she snuggled him into bed beside her.

Who cares! he agreed.

'I know what I heard in that computer room!'

Uh-huh. You know what I think?

'No, what?'

I think Nathan's scared stiff of Winona fancying him. That's why he refused to help you.

Daisy thought it through. 'Yeah, Winona did come on a bit strong,' she recalled.

And Winona's sulking because of how Nathan blanked her.

'You're right, Herb. But what about Jimmy? He believes everything I tell him, and even *he* told me to get lost!'

Jimmy just wants to have a good time at Highfield, Herbie pointed out. *But hey, listen – I believe you!*

Good old Herbie! Daisy sighed and settled him into a cosier position. 'Bernie wants the City manager to steal Robbie Exley!' she confided. 'He wants us to lose the Premiership!'

We won't let him, Herbie promised. He was drifting off to sleep, only half hearing what Daisy said.

'No, we won't let him!' Daisy agreed, tossing and turning for a bit. Then she settled and stared up at the ceiling. 'We're gonna stop him!' she promised.

Zzzz!

Daisy didn't notice that Herbie had nodded off. 'This is the plan...' she said.

Thirteen

'Daisy, what are you doing?' her mum asked early next morning.

She'd caught Daisy hiding under the kitchen table, taking photos of Mia with her dad's digital camera.

'Ssssh! Pretend I'm not here!' Daisy hissed.

Click! She got one of Mia spitting out a spoonful of stewed apple and custard mush. *Click, click!* She captured Mia squawking for more. Right – time to make an exit! Slithering along on her belly, Daisy made for the door.

'I can see you, Daisy!' her mum said, without turning her head.

Rats! Daisy froze, then rolled on to her back and quickly pressed the secret button on her wristwatch. The watch turned into a mini gun and she aimed and fired. *Zap!* Her mum was history.

101

'Daisy, you're going to be late for soccer school!' Angie sighed, wiping Mia's mouth and carrying the empty bowl to the sink.

There was a bright light shining into her eyes. Her hands were tied behind her back, her mouth was gagged.

Agent 0077 was in a tough spot.

'Who are you working for?' a woman's voice asked.

The light blinded her, but 0077 knew they were on a luxury boat, somewhere in the Caribbean. She felt the rise and fall of the waves, heard the purr of the engines. 'You'll get nothing out of me, lady!' she grunted through her gag.

Someone untied the gag then tilted the light away from her eyes. 'Come on, Miss Morelli, we don't have time to play games!'

0077 blinked. She worked secretly at the knot tying her hands, felt it coming loose behind her back.

'We caught you taking digital pictures of our plans to take over the world!' the tough-talking woman warned. 'We need to know who your bosses are!'

Gradually 0077 made out the face across the table. It was a face she'd known all her life – big brown eyes, long dark hair, full lips. 'Mum!' she gasped.

'Yes, Daisy!' Angie sneered. 'I know you didn't suspect me, but I'm going to take over the world, and nothing you do will stop me!'

'Says you!' 0077 snapped back, freeing her hands and springing to her feet. With one mighty swing of her leg, she kick-boxed the enemy to the ground, sat on her chest and used the rope to tie her up.

'OK, you win!' Angie gasped.

'Give me the plans!' 0077 demanded, ready with a kung-fu chop.

'In the table drawer!' her mum whined.

Quickly Daisy seized the papers and leaped upstairs on to the boat deck. The sea was blue, the sky clear. There was a warm breeze blowing.

0077 held up the evil plans for world destruction. She let the breeze catch them, felt them flutter in her fingers, then released them.

The wind caught the papers, carried them, then let them fall into the clear water, where they floated then sank, one by one, into the depths of the ocean.

'Dad, can I borrow your camera?' Daisy asked.

Her mum was right – she was going to be late. But she needed to take a few extra items into Highfield on this last but one day of her training course.

'Daisy, I'm not happy.' Her dad shook his head as he chopped onions. 'This camera is expensive.'

'I won't break it, I promise!' she pleaded.

'Do you know how it works?'

''Course! Dad, say yes, ple-ease!'

Chop-chop, slice, scoop into the pan. *Sizzle.*

'I want to take pictures of the other kids on the course!' Daisy fibbed. 'And of Gary and Kevin Crowe. I might even get one of Robbie and get him to sign it!'

Sizzle, sigh. 'I don't know, Daisy *mia*!'

Daisy made her lip wobble and sniffed in the scent of raw onions to get her eyes to water. 'I might never get a chance like this ever again!' she whimpered.

'OK, yes, take the camera!' Her dad gave in with a grin. 'But take good care of it!'

'Cool, thanks!' Daisy sped away before he could change his mind.

'OK, I've got a camera, a magnifying glass, a pen with invisible ink and some rope to tie people up with!' Daisy announced in the Highfield changing room. Everyone else had gone on to the pitch to start warming up for training.

Jimmy looked up from fastening his boots. 'Yeah, whatever,' he muttered.

'Jimmy, this is serious! Bernie King is spying for Ashby City. We have to stop him!'

'Hm.'

'What d'you mean, "hm"?'

Jimmy shoved his shin pads down his socks. 'Back off, Daisy, I'm busy.'

'Don't you care?' she demanded. 'Do you actually want Robbie to leave Steelers and play for City? Do you want us to lose the Premiership?'

''Course not,' Jimmy grunted. 'But it's not gonna happen.'

Daisy frowned as she stuffed her bag into her locker. 'I thought you were my mate,' she sniffed.

Taking a deep breath, then jogging on the spot, Jimmy refused to be sucked in. 'Sure we're mates,' he said, 'but that doesn't mean I have to go along with everything you say.'

Daisy slammed the metal door. 'Fine,' she grunted.

'Does it?' he insisted.

She stormed ahead, down the corridor, past the room where the ground staff were drinking tea.

'Does it?' Jimmy said yet again, trotting to keep up.

'No, it's cool!' Daisy insisted through gritted teeth. 'I'll do it myself. I'll spy on Bernie and Mr Waymann without anyone helping me. Winona and Nathan refused, and you as well, Jimmy. But it's cool!'

Jimmy frowned and put on a sprint. 'Cool!' he said, bursting ahead of Daisy. 'I'm cool if you're cool. C'mon, let's play footie!'

'This is so *not* cool!' Daisy confessed to Herbie during

the mid-morning break. 'No one believes me, yet I know I'm right!'

'Daisy, put more effort into it!' Gary had yelled at her during warm-up. Her press-ups were half-hearted. She was thinking of other things.

'OK, now find a partner!' the coach instructed. Jimmy rushed to team up with the red-haired kid from Marshway Juniors and Daisy got stuck with Darren Longlegs.

'Daisy Morelli, did you leave your brains behind today?' Gary taunted after she scored an own goal in the five-a-side practice match.

Pants! she'd groaned to herself. *Pants, pants, pants!*

And now they were having a break. Jimmy was chatting to Carrot-top and Daisy had taken Herbie on her visit to the loo. She sat on the closed lid, arms crossed, nattering away.

'Did you see the way Bernie looked at me when I was getting into trouble?' she asked. 'You could tell he was enjoying it!'

No, I was stuck in your bag inside your locker, remember?

Daisy ignored him. 'The thing is, I'm dead worried about Robbie. We don't want to lose him. I mean, Steelers needs Robbie Exley like...like a fish needs water! And I just caught Bernie Sneaky King whispering with Mr Waymann again-'

Hold it! Herbie said, cutting her short. *Why don't you quit complaining and do something?*

Daisy gasped then stood up. 'You're right!' she said, stuffing Herbie in her pocket and unlocking the door. 'It's time for action. If proof is what they want, then proof is what they're gonna get!'

Daisy tiptoed down corridors and slid silently around corners. She held her dad's camera firmly in one hand.

'How are the kids doing?' Kevin Crowe was asking Gary Ford as Daisy stopped outside the manager's door.

'They're doing great,' Gary told him. 'I'd like a couple of them to come back on a regular basis.'

Daisy held her breath.

'Well, we have room for three or four on the junior programme,' Kevin said. 'If you pick the best of this week's bunch, I'll write to their parents and invite them to join us.'

Wow! Daisy's eyes lit up. Just wait until she told the rest. But that would come later. Right now, she was a spy.

She snuck on, found the computer room and peeked inside. *Result!* There was Michael Waymann working on his laptop, with Bernie King looking over his shoulder. Daisy pressed herself against the wall and listened in.

'So, how often do they do a drugs test on a top professional footballer?' Bernie was asking in a dead casual way.

Mr Waymann tapped his keyboard. 'That depends,' he answered quietly.

'Every week?' Bernie persisted.

'Oh no, nothing like so often as that.'

Why does Bernie want to know? Daisy wondered, whipping out a pad and her invisible ink pen and scribbling rapid notes.

'And what happens if a top player fails to show up for a pre-match training session? Does he get dropped from the team?'

'Sometimes,' came the slow reply.

Daisy frowned. What she needed was a quick photo of the two men together. This would be her first piece of proof that they were plotting bad things for Robbie. It was a pity she couldn't record their conversation, but her invisible notes would have to do.

'Listen, I want you to post an item about Robbie on the website for me,' Bernie went on, leaning forward and muttering something which Daisy couldn't pick up.

Right, this was it! As the two men were busy, she stepped into the doorway, raised her camera, aimed and clicked.

'You're late!' Gary grumbled. He'd already picked his teams for another five-a-side trial when Daisy got back to the training pitch after the break for orange juice and biscuits. 'You'll have to go over to the main stand and sit this one out.'

Glumly Daisy trailed off to the neighbouring pitch, where members of the Steelers squad were practising for next day's match. *At least I get to watch Robbie!* she told herself. *And I got my picture!*

'*Grrrr!*' Lennox growled as she passed him. Across the pitch, Lennox's owner and another groundsman were cleaning the bright electronic signs that lined the front edge of the far stand.

'Who let you in?' she muttered. Wow, was that an ugly dog!

'*Grrrr!*' came the reply.

Ugly, as in drooling lips, saggy cheeks and big bags under the eyes. Ugly, as in fat belly and short, stumpy legs, with chunky black leather collar studded with steel spikes.

Lennox is a punk! Daisy pictured the bad-breath bulldog with pierced ears and a stud in his nose. She grinned then glanced at the players on the pitch, picking out her hero's light blond hair and trademark white boots. *Hey, wait a doggone minute!* She thought about Lennox again – that collar, those studs!

With eyes narrowed, Daisy crept slowly towards Lennox. 'Here, boy!' she whispered. 'Nice doggy, here, boy!'

'*Werruff!*' The dog gave a low, warning bark.

On the pitch, Kevin Crowe yelled at Marc Predoux to pass to Robbie.

'Here, Lennox, let me stroke you. I only want an ickle look at your lovely collar!'

'*Werrrruuufff!*' A louder bark made Bernie glance up from his Kit-Kat ad.

'Just one little look. C'mon, I know what you've got there!' Daisy murmured. 'You can't fool me! There's a secret camera fixed inside one of those metal studs, and you're sitting there filming Steelers' tactics for tomorrow!'

By now she could feel Lennox's hot, nasty breath on her outstretched hand.

'*Grrr-werruff!*' He growl-barked. *Wumph!* He turned his head quick as a flash, opened his jaws and slammed them shut.

'Ouch!' Daisy snatched her hand away in the nick of time.

'Someone get rid of that dog!' the Steelers manager yelled, and Bernie jogged heavily around the edge of the pitch to haul his bulldog away.

'They were filming Robbie in training!' Daisy whispered to Jimmy at lunchtime. She'd cornered him by the fizzy drinks machine and made him listen. 'There was a secret camera in Lennox's collar. Listen to me, Jimmy!'

'I'm listening,' Jimmy said, swilling 7-Up around his mouth, tipping his head back and taking a big swallow.

'Bernie was filming Robbie, right! He's gonna sell the secret video to City so they can work out our tactics for Saturday's match!'

'Bad news,' Jimmy mumbled. He shook the can to fizz it up then took another big gulp.

'Anyway, at least I got Lennox out of the way,' Daisy reminded herself how Kevin had shown the dog a red card. 'But it won't stop Bernie trying all sorts of other dodgy stuff!'

Jimmy trickled the last drops of drink into his mouth then stamped on the can and chucked it in the bin. 'You're nuts, you know that?' he told her.

Then Darren wandered by with a *Helston Herald* in his hand. 'Have you heard the latest?' he asked, waving the newspaper at them. 'They're saying that Robbie might not be fit for Saturday's match.'

'Huh? How come?' Jimmy stood still for two whole seconds while Daisy grabbed the paper and turned to the sports page.

'"Fitness Query over Robbie!"' she read out loud. '"According to information picked up on the Steelers' official website this morning, there is a serious question over ace-scorer Robbie Exley's match fitness. Insiders at Highfield have admitted that several members of the squad have gone down with a mystery virus, and Robbie Exley may be one of them..."'

'B-but!' Jimmy stammered.

'It's the first I heard of it!' Darren added with a shrug.

'But don't you see?' Daisy squeaked, her heart thudding. 'You know who's behind this, don't you? This is another dirty trick by that low-down, no-good spy, Bernie King!'

Fourteen

'You're nuts, Daisy!' Jimmy said again. He went off laughing with Darren.

Daisy followed glumly. How could she make them understand?

'Hey kids, you're in for a special treat this afternoon!' Gary announced when they'd all gathered on the training pitch. 'The first-team squad is going to join us again for a warm-up session, so be on your toes and show them what you can do!'

Yeah! Every single member of the soccer school, including Daisy, grinned and punched the air.

'Tell me I'm not dreaming!' Darren declared.

Jimmy jumped around like a mad grasshopper. 'Yeah!' he cried.

And before they knew it, Kevin Crowe was leading his team out. The lads from the first team came on to the pitch laughing and joking, tapping balls between them, occasionally stopping to bend and stretch.

'Hi!' Kevin greeted the youngsters. 'Are you ready for a real workout?'

'Cool!' they crowed, jiggling and jogging, tapping and passing like the first-team squad.

There was Marc Predoux with his trendy corn-row locks; Lyndon Simons, the recent signing who everyone said was the new Robbie Exley. Daisy nearly choked with excitement when Lyndon passed a ball to her.

Then she spotted Pedro Martinez teaming up with Jimmy, and the Steelers' great goalie, Hans Kohl, chatting with Darren. *This is so cool!* Daisy told herself. All her heroes were here ...

'You're doing a great job,' Kevin Crowe said to Daisy.

She turned and beamed at him.

'I've been very impressed by your footballing skills,' the manager told her. 'You read the game well.'

'Thanks,' Daisy said, blushing to the roots of her tangled hair.

Kevin nodded. 'Would you like to come back to

Highfield and hang out with the Juniors?'

Daisy felt weak at the knees. All she could do was nod back before Kevin Crowe moved on to talk to someone else.

'Swing low, sweet char-i-ot…!' A crowd of a hundred thousand Steelers supporters sang for Daisy Morelli.

She held the Cup above her head and jogged round the pitch.

'Swi-ing low, sweet char-i-ot…!'

'Daisy, what did he say?' Jimmy hissed, breaking into Daisy's best dream ever.

'I'm coming back to Highfield!' Daisy sighed. 'Kevin Crowe likes my footballing skills. Jimmy, is that cool, or what!'

'Yeah,' her best mate said, dropping his head to hide his own disappointment. 'Yeah, Daisy, that's great. I'm glad for you…nice one.'

And then it was more running and receiving, tackling and passing.

They were ten minutes into the mega training session before Daisy saw what she

should have seen in the first ten seconds. All her heroes were here except...

'Where's Robbie?' she asked Darren.

Robbie with the blond stubble and the broad shoulders, Robbie with his soft white boots and superb body swerve. Her superhero, Robbie.

Darren shrugged.

Daisy felt a shock jolt through her like an electric current. Why wasn't Robbie Exley with the squad? And why was Bernie King at the side of the pitch with his nephew, William, the two of them standing with their arms crossed, laughing, with Lennox squatting beside them?

Too many questions, and Daisy needed some answers!

'OK, lads, take a break!' Kevin called his squad off the pitch, while Gary gathered the kids for a tactical talk.

'It's what I was talking about earlier!' Daisy hissed at Jimmy, huddling up close so no one could hear. 'Robbie's not here. Bernie King got to him!'

Jimmy bit his lip. 'Maybe Robbie's busy,' he muttered.

'No way! Robbie wouldn't miss training. Bernie King got to him!'

'Meaning what?' Jimmy wanted to know.

'Meaning, he probably put something in Robbie's drink to make him feel sick, so he misses Saturday's match! I heard him talking to Mr Waymann about drugs and stuff!'

'Oh wow!' Jimmy sighed. There was a troubled look in his eye.

'Look at Bernie now!' Daisy warned.

Their school caretaker was laughing out loud with William, pointing his stubby finger at Daisy, and laughing again.

Jimmy frowned. 'Wow, Daisy!' was all he could say.

She could tell that he was starting to believe her at last. 'Then there's the rumour in the paper about Robbie's fitness – Bernie made Mr Waymann put that out on the website – I heard him! And I've got a picture of them together, if you want to see it.'

'What are we gonna do?' Jimmy croaked. All of a sudden he realised what was happening with Bernie and Mr Waymann and Ashby City and panic set in. 'C'mon, Daisy, we've got to tell Kevin!'

'No, wait!' she hissed. 'OK, so Bernie's a spy, and we know it. But he could deny it. He could just laugh it off, like grown-ups always do!'

Jimmy groaned. 'So what now?'

Daisy leaned even closer. 'You see Lennox? You remember the secret camera in his collar I told you about?'

Her friend nodded, his eyes wide as a scared rabbit's.

'I bet it's still there!' Daisy told him. She put her lips against Jimmy's ear. 'It's a mini spy camera and I'm going to get it off him!'

'Wow!' Jimmy breathed. He turned to stare at Fat Lennox, the heavyweight champion of bulldogs, muscles bulging, fat chops slobbering. He shook his head. 'It's way too risky,' he muttered.

'We need that collar!' Daisy insisted. She'd tried once and failed. But this time, slobbery jaws or not, she would succeed.

'Don't do it!' Jimmy begged. But he knew deep down that nothing he said to Daisy Angelina Morelli would stop her from doing what she had to do.

Fifteen

Daisy scoffed her tea as fast as she could.

'Don't gobble!' her mum warned. 'You'll do yourself an injury.'

Too late – Daisy's plate was empty. 'I'm off to Jimmy's,' she gabbled, scraping her chair on the tiles as she stood up and hurtled out of the kitchen.

'Don't you see enough of Jimmy during the day?' Angie inquired, her voice trailing off as Daisy shot out of the back door.

Jimmy and Daisy had arranged to meet up outside his dad's Carworld shop at six o'clock. Daisy was to bring her 0077 equipment – camera, magnifying glass and piece of rope. Jimmy, for his part, had promised to stash some tasty food from supper, pop it into a doggy bag and bring it along.

He was there waiting, still dressed in his blue Steelers shirt and white shorts. He looked pale and worried. 'Are you sure about this?' he asked Daisy when she squealed to a halt.

'Yeah, c'mon!' No time to think. When you were a spy, you had to act fast.

So they sprinted to Woodbridge Road in record time – past the park where Winona was walking Mimi, past a row of shops, round the corner and on to the street where their school stood.

'Hold it!' Jimmy gasped.

They stopped by the high stone wall surrounding the playground. 'There's Bernie's car!' Daisy pointed to a silver hatchback parked outside the school gate. 'That means he's back home!'

The caretaker lived in a small, new house behind the school. It stood in its own garden, with a clear view of the tall, old school building and the playground.

'We have to get across the playground without him seeing us,' Jimmy reminded Daisy.

'Yeah, let's think about this. What time is it? Quarter past six. Bernie's probably watching the news on telly.'

'Or having his tea,' Jimmy suggested.

Daisy drew a deep breath. 'Right, we'll climb the

OK?'

She had one leg over the top of the high iron gate, ready to swing the other one over when Jimmy spoke.

'Look who's coming!'

Daisy glanced down the street, and who did she see but Curly-Whirly Winona prancing along with her precious pooch!

'Mind you don't fall, Daisy!' Winona called, sounding just like Miss Ambler. 'I saw you from the park. What are you doing? No, don't tell me – you're spying on Mr King!'

'Sssssshhhhh!' Daisy hissed.

'We're busted!' Jimmy groaned.

'What have you got in that bag, Jimmy?' Winona chirped. 'And Daisy, why have you got a rope slung across your shoulder?'

'*Rrrufff!*' Mimi chipped in.

'We're not spying!' Daisy retorted. 'I left something in my classroom drawer. I'm just going to fetch it.'

'School's locked!' Winona declared with a know-it-all grin.

Daisy glared down at her.

Agent 0077 knew she couldn't talk her way out of this one. The blonde was on to her.

Yet she'd come a long way on this mission. She'd flown a

plane into a mountain and parachuted to safety. She'd crashed a tank into a wall, then jumped from a cliff into the sea, stolen a speedboat and escaped. Now she was close to finding the secret information she needed. It was there, in that dog's collar – a camera smaller than a five pence coin, with all the evidence she needed. If only this girl with the curls would get out of the way.

'Do us a favour, lady,' 0077 drawled. 'Go polish your fingernails. Get out of my hair.'

The blonde smiled back. 'Who's gonna make me?'

'Get lost, Winona!' Jimmy grunted.

'Why should I?'

'*Rruff!*' Mimi agreed.

Daisy climbed down from the gate. 'Run!' she said to Jimmy.

They legged it down Woodbridge Road, trying to lose Winona. Winona stuck close, back into the park, across the grass, behind some bushes and around the duck pond.

'I'm not leaving until you've told me what you're up to,' Little Ms Superglue insisted.

'OK, OK!' Daisy cried. 'We are spying on Bernie, if you must know! But if you tell anyone, you're dead!'

'I knew it!' Winona said with a smirk.

The second time Daisy climbed the school gate, she

had Jimmy plus Winona, plus Mimi in tow.

'We'll help!' Winona had decided.

'Who's "we"?' Daisy sulked.

'Me and Mimi.'

'No, you won't,' Daisy groaned.

'Yes, we will. Come on, Daisy, come on, Jimmy, we're wasting time arguing!' And Winona had marched ahead, back towards the school.

'If that dog barks and gives us away, I'll strangle it!' Daisy muttered now. She jumped down into the playground and waited for the others to follow.

The pesky poodle squeezed under the gate and scampered ahead.

'Here, Mimi!' Winona trilled as she scaled the gate in her new white cut-offs and pale pink top.

The dog waited then trotted at her heel.

'What do you have in mind for making Lennox come outside?' Winona whispered to Daisy as they pressed themselves against the wall of the Infants building and peered around the corner at Bernie's house.

Daisy pointed to the bag of food in Jimmy's hand.

'Sausage and beans!' he hissed, holding up the squidgy mess.

'Yuck!' Winona wrinkled her nose.

Mimi sniffed at the bag then turned away in disgust.

'Then what?' Winona wanted to know.

'Lennox smells the food and comes out to snaffle it,' Daisy explained. 'I've got this rope, see. I lasso it round Lennox's neck while he's busy eating. Then Jimmy moves in. He undoes the buckle on the collar, grabs it, then we leg it.'

'What's that for?' Winona asked, pointing to the camera around Daisy's neck.

Daisy shrugged. 'Just in case we need it.'

'Give it to me,' Winona told her, holding out her hand. 'I'll take pictures. Come on, let's go!'

So they edged forward, crouching and creeping low towards Bernie King's garden gate.

'*Yip!*' Mimi yelped when Daisy accidentally stood on her toe.

'Sssshushh!' Daisy, Jimmy and Winona warned.

They crept closer. Now they could hear a telly playing through the open window of a downstairs room. 'The prime minister flew to Japan today as part of his policy to improve relations…blah-blah…'

'Hey, the front door's open!' Jimmy pointed to a gap in the door. He got ready with the food. 'But how do we make Lennox come outside?' he frowned. 'If we make a noise, Bernie's bound to hear us and come out too.'

'Hmmm. Maybe Lennox'll smell the sausages.' For the first time Daisy saw a slight flaw in her plan. How to separate the dog from the man? This wasn't going to be easy.

'I know!' Winona said brightly. 'We stay here, hiding behind the fence, while Mimi goes to fetch Lennox!'

Without giving Daisy time to think, she leaned forward to whisper in the poodle's ear. 'Go on, Mimi. Go find Lennox!'

The dog obeyed, squeezing under Bernie's gate then trotting prettily up to the front door.

'Sssh, Mimi!' Winona warned.

Daisy and Jimmy held their breaths. What if Mimi barked? Then they truly would be busted. Jimmy put one hand over his eyes, not daring to look.

Sniff-sniff! Mimi padded around Lennox's front step. She poked her dainty black nose through the gap in the door.

'What if Lennox grabs her and gobbles her up?' Daisy breathed.

'He won't!' Winona said, with a calm smile.

'*Heruff!,* Bernie's bulldog came snuffling to the door. He spotted Mimi and wagged his stumpy tail. Then he came out on to the path and pushed his slobbery chops into the poodle's face.

'Beauty and the Beast!' Daisy whispered.

'See, he likes her!' Winona smirked. 'Here, Mimi, come back to mummy!'

Yuck! Daisy felt her lip curl, but still she had to hand it to Winona – her plan to lure Lennox out of the house was working perfectly.

Mimi came, closely followed by Lennox.

'Cool. Now show him the beans and sausages!' Daisy whispered to Jimmy. She, Winona and Jimmy were still hidden behind Bernie's fence, but Lennox must have caught their scent. He cocked his head to one side and paused before he followed Mimi through the gate.

'The sausages, Jimmy!' Daisy hissed again.

Jimmy opened the bag and inched forward. 'Here, Lennox, yummy food!' he muttered.

Lennox sniffed hard. He fixed Jimmy with his droopy eyes.

Jimmy trembled. Lennox was only a metre away, and from here his teeth looked big and sharp. 'Are you ready to g-g-grab him?' he asked Daisy.

She nodded. Meanwhile, Winona picked Mimi up. 'Stay here with mummy,' she cooed. 'Keep out of that nasty big dog's way!'

Still glaring at Jimmy, Fat Lennox inched towards the tempting treat.

'Lovely, yummy, scrummy sausages!' Jimmy squeaked, his hand shaking so much that he almost dropped the treat.

Lennox sniffed and drooled. He poked his blunt nose into the bag.

'Now!' Jimmy yelped.

Daisy sprang forward from a crouched-frog position. She landed with both arms around Lennox's neck.

'*Warrrufff!*' Lennox snarled, shaking Daisy until her teeth rattled.

Daisy rolled sideways, hoping to drag Lennox with her. But the bulldog was super-strong. He stayed on his feet and turned for home.

'Come back!' Jimmy hissed, waving the sausages at the retreating dog.

Daisy held tight, but she couldn't stop Lennox. He dragged her into the garden.

'Get his collar!' Jimmy called.

'I'm trying!' Daisy yelled back. Unhooking the rope from her shoulder, she slipped one end under the collar and fought Lennox as he hauled her into Bernie's rose bed. 'Ouch! Ouch!' Pink and yellow petals showered down on her.

'Ooh, those thorns!' Winona sighed, taking a sneak picture through a gap in the fence and shaking her head.

Then Daisy and Lennox were through the roses and on to Bernie's smooth green lawn. Daisy had her fingers on the buckle of the precious collar. Five more seconds and she would have it off.

'Poor Daisy. It's like wrestling a bull!' Jimmy breathed.

'*Warruff! Wrrrrufff!*' Lennox fought to free himself from Daisy's grasp.

'What's all this racket?' At the sound of Lennox barking, Bernie came roaring out of the house at last. He saw a ruined rose bed and Daisy clinging like a limpet to his dog.

Winona ducked lower, clutching Mimi close. Jimmy jumped up to warn Daisy.

The caretaker paused for a split second. It was long enough for Daisy to finally wrench the collar from Lennox's neck and fling it up into the air.

The collar flew towards Jimmy, who caught it.

'Run, Jimmy!' Daisy yelled, catching a glimpse of Bernie's trouser legs and big boots from under Lennox's belly. She let go of the dog and lay sprawled on the grass.

Jimmy sprinted across the playground.

'Fetch him, Lennox!' Bernie bellowed, darting towards Daisy, who was too quick for him. She twisted out of the caretaker's reach, jumped up and hurdled the garden fence.

Then Winona stood up and presented herself calmly to the caretaker. 'I know!' she sighed, stroking Mimi and standing in the gateway so that Lennox trundled to a halt. 'It's awful, isn't it? Daisy's up to her usual tricks!'

Bernie stood with his arms folded, a deep frown creasing his forehead. 'What do you know about this?' he asked.

Winona smiled. 'Nothing,' she said with a toss of her curls. 'Only that Daisy Disaster Morelli is in trouble yet again!'

Sixteen

'I was only trying to help!' Winona complained.

'Yeah, yeah, yeah!' Daisy grunted. She and Jimmy were examining Lennox's collar, turning it this way and that. 'I heard what you said!'

'It worked, didn't it?' Winona frowned. 'Mimi and I stopped Bernie and Lennox from chasing you.'

Jimmy, Daisy and Winona had met up in the park, five minutes after Operation Sausages.

'What do you reckon Bernie'll do?' Jimmy said.

'Phone Mrs Waymann,' Winona told them calmly. 'Hey, do you want to see this picture I took of you and Lennox?'

'No!' Daisy winced and picked another rose thorn from her shin. 'Ouch!'

'Here, let me look at that!' Winona said, snatching Lennox's collar from Jimmy. She studied it carefully. 'So where's this mini-camera then?'

'Here, give it to me!' Daisy seized the collar and inspected the steel studs. 'There must be a tiny lens here somewhere.'

Winona arched her eyebrows.

'Not there...not there...' One by one, Daisy examined the studs until she came to the last in the row.

'So?' Jimmy prompted.

Daisy gritted her teeth. 'Nothing,' she admitted.

'No camera?' Jimmy's voice fell flat.

'Whoops!' Winona smirked.

Daisy let the collar dangle from her hand. She was scratched and pricked all over, covered in dirt. And all for nothing. 'OK, so it was only a guess,' she admitted. 'Bernie King must have found some other way of spying on Steelers!'

'Or else you were wrong about him in the first place,' Winona argued, as the ducks on the duck pond swam up to eat the portions of cold sausage and beans that Jimmy had just fed them.

'I know I'm right!' Daisy frowned. 'Bernie's most likely taking notes on everything that Kevin Crowe does in training, and passing them on to the City trainer. He probably gets Mr Waymann to e-mail them.'

'*Quack!*' The ducks ducked and jostled in the water. *Gulp-gulp!*

'Look, they like beans!' Jimmy said.

'*Ruff!*' Mimi barked. She darted to the edge of the pond.

'That's a very scary dog you've got there!' Daisy muttered sarcastically. 'Winona, you've got to take this collar back to Bernie and explain it was all a mistake. Ask him not to ring Waymann.'

'Who says I've got to?' Winona wanted to know.

'...Ple-ease!' Daisy whinged.

'Only if you promise to follow my new plan!' Winona replied, speaking slowly and making Daisy follow her every word.

'Keep your hair on, Nathan,' Daisy protested. 'This wasn't my idea!'

It was seven o'clock. Winona had trotted back to Bernie King's to hand over Lennox's collar. Then Daisy, Jimmy, Winona and Mimi had trekked up to Nathan's house on the hill.

'This sounds like another of your stupid plans,' Nathan sighed, ready to close the door on Daisy and the others.

'Hey, Einstein, it's your girlfriend and her two mates,' Luke crowed as he barged into the house. 'Nathan's pulled!' he announced in a loud voice to their mum and dad.

Nathan scowled and blushed. 'Get lost!' he told his visitors.

Winona elbowed Daisy and Jimmy out of the way. 'Nathan, listen,' she insisted. 'All we want you to do is hack into Mr Waymann's laptop!'

'Oh cool!' Nathan scoffed.

'It was my idea, actually,' Winona went on, treating Nathan to one of her sweetest smiles. 'We need someone really clever to help us. I mean, Daisy's a spy, but she's not a very good one...'

'Hey!' Daisy protested.

'...Like I say, we need a person with brains who knows a lot about computers.'

'And Winona thought of you!' Jimmy explained. 'You're so brainy, Nathan, they're just about busting out of your head.'

'Yeah, and Bernie's been getting Mr Waymann to e-mail messages to the Ashby City coach!' Daisy broke in. 'I've got a photo of them together in the IT room at Highfield. And now Robbie's gone missing, and we know that Bernie's either drugged him or kidnapped him!'

'We do?' Winona and Jimmy queried.

'Yes, we do. This is a big plot to get rid of Robbie and stop Steelers winning the Premiership,' Daisy insisted. 'Where was he this afternoon? Why did he miss training?'

'Because he didn't feel well?' Nathan came in with a sensible suggestion.

'Exactly!' Daisy cried. 'Bernie drugged him! But we still need proof, and that's why you have to hack Waymann's computer.'

'Hack *into*,' Winona corrected.

'We could smuggle you into Highfield with us tomorrow,' Jimmy explained. 'It's our last day, so we need to work fast.'

'Yeah, and it's the big match on Saturday.' Daisy too knew that they had to get a move on. 'Steelers play City in the deciding match for the Premiership!'

'Run that by me again?' Nathan muttered. 'You said, *smuggle me into Highfield?*'

'Yeah, or sneak into Waymann's place tonight!' Daisy sprang this one on them all. It hadn't been part of Winona's original plan. *Just call me brilliant!* she thought.

'Yes, Nathan!' Winona agreed eagerly. 'We know where Mrs Waymann lives. It should be easy for Jimmy and me to keep her and Mr Waymann busy at the front door while you and Daisy sneak round the back!'

'But I *never* do anything naughty!' Nathan complained.

Daisy grinned. It was true – Nathan was the class geek who always did as he was told. Now he was a spy, about to break into the Headteacher's house. 'Don't worry, Einstein, you'll soon get used to it,' she assured him.

'You're so-ooh clever, Nathan!' Winona cooed. 'I bet you could hack into any computer system in the world!'

Nathan shrugged. 'I expect I could.'

'And you won't get found out,' Daisy promised. 'We'll cover for you.'

'What's in it for me?' Nathan asked.

'He's giving in!' Daisy hissed at Jimmy.

'The glory of saving Robbie Exley!' Winona said.

'We are members of a spy network fighting to save the free world!' Agent 0077 explained to Professor Moss. She had found him in his science lab, busy splitting atoms. 'If you join us, your name will go down in history!'

The prof looked up from his test tubes. His white coat was stained with chemicals, his glasses cracked and taped together with an Elastoplast.

Definitely a mad professor type, 0077 thought. But we need people like him on our side! 'We'll also pay you ten million pounds,' she offered.

'I'll give you a fiver if you help us,' Daisy said. It was worth the five pounds she had left in her piggy bank after paying for Winona's new trousers to rescue Robbie from Bernie's evil clutches.

'OK, it's a deal!' Nathan decided on the spot.

So now they were making for the Waymanns' house on Lilac Avenue.

'Tell me again, what are we gonna say when we knock on the door?' Jimmy asked Winona as they approached the big house behind the tall beech hedge.

'We're going to ask them both to come out into the front garden so we can take their photograph with you, Jimmy,' Winona reminded him. 'I'm going to say that it's for an article I'm writing for the school magazine.'

'About me going to Kevin's academy,' Jimmy recalled. 'Yeah, got it!'

'And that's when you and I sneak around the back of the house, go in and find Mr Waymann's laptop,' Daisy told Nathan.

'What if the back is all locked up?' Nathan wanted to know. Suddenly he felt that five pounds was chicken feed for the risk he was about to take.

'It won't be,' Daisy assured him.

'What if it is?'

'Nathan, read my lips. It…won't…be!' He was such a wimp!

'Right!' Winona stopped by the Waymanns' gate.

Peeking through the hedge, Daisy recognised the winding gravel drive, the stone porch and the rambling ivy up the front of the house.

'Everybody ready?' Winona asked.

'One-two, one-two, right-left, right-left!' Sergeant-Major Jones made her troops march up the hill and down again. Her brass buttons sparkled, her black boots shone.

'Private Black, get into line! Private Morelli, no slouching! Corporal Moss; straighten up that rifle! About turn!'

'Ready!' the others whispered meekly.

Winona checked the camera, then tied Mimi to the gatepost. 'Wait here!' she told the poodle. *Left-right-left* – she and Jimmy marched up the drive.

'I'll do it for a tenner!' Nathan hissed at Daisy as they peered through the hedge.

'You said five!' she muttered back.

'Seven pounds fifty?'

'Deal!' she said through clenched teeth, as Winona knocked at the door and Mr Waymann appeared. Robbie was worth it, even if she had to work to earn money in her dad's restaurant for the whole summer!

'Mr Waymann!' Winona said, flashing the Head's husband a bright white smile. 'I'm sorry to bother you during half-term, but is Mrs Waymann in? We'd like to talk to her!'

'Phew, she's so good!' Daisy admitted. Winona spun a story better than anyone she knew.

Mousy Mr Waymann was dressed in dark blue tracksuit bottoms and a white polo shirt. 'What's it about?' he asked with a kindly smile.

Winona sold him the guff about her magazine article. 'It's thanks to you and Mrs Waymann that Jimmy got to go to the Academy,' she said sweetly. 'Everyone in Woodbridge Road Juniors would love to read about it!'

At Winona's side, Jimmy hopped nervously from one foot to the other. He spotted the dreaded Head approaching down the hallway.

Mrs Waymann was in a holiday mood. She wore a lime-green flowered top with long orange shorts and white flip-flops. 'Hello, Winona!' she said as she appeared beside Mr Waymann.

'Cor, reach for the sunglasses!' Daisy whispered from behind the hedge. 'Bright shirt, or what!'

Before long Winona had managed to tempt both grown-ups out on to the lawn and Jimmy was lined up in between them for a photo shoot.

'This is it!' Daisy hissed to Nathan, leading him silently down the side of the garden. Then she went down on her hands and knees and crept through a gap in the hedge.

'What if someone sees us?' Nathan squeaked. They'd come through on to a vegetable patch, into the middle of Mr Waymann's lettuces.

'Are you a man or a mouse?' Daisy demanded. She spied an open French door leading on to a patio. So far, Operation Lilac Avenue was going according to plan...

'Smile for the camera!' Winona chirruped. She aimed and clicked as Mr and Mrs Waymann grinned cheesily on the front lawn and Jimmy stretched his mouth into a fake grin. 'Oops!' she cried. 'It didn't work. I'll have to do it again. Look this way, please. Now, smile!'...

'Follow me!' Daisy told Nathan. They were inside the house. It was stuffed full of armchairs and ornaments, vases of flowers, gold-framed pictures and gleaming mirrors.

'I d-d-don't like this!' Nathan breathed.

Daisy ignored him. 'Now, where's that laptop?' she wondered...

'Oh dear, I don't think this camera is working!' Winona sighed. She'd decided to act the helpless girlie and play for time. 'Mr Waymann, can you tell me what I should be pressing? Is this the button for taking the picture, or is it this one?'

'So, Jimmy, how have you got on at Highfield?' Mrs Waymann asked, to pass the time while her husband went to help Winona.

'G-g-good!' Jimmy croaked. 'We had our p-p-picture taken with R-R-Robbie Exley!' He was talking to the Head, stumbling and stammering over his words, trying to keep her from wandering back into the house. Help, what could he say! 'Robbie's c-c-cool!' he added.

'Come along, Michael, what's the problem?' Mrs Waymann called impatiently.

'Nothing dear. I'm just explaining how to work the camera,' he called back. 'You see, Winona, it's really simple – you just get the picture up on this tiny screen and press this button…'

'Here it is!' Daisy cried. She pounced on the laptop computer which sat on a low table by the French window. 'C'mon, Nathan, start hacking!'

'I'm not hacking!' he said crossly, wiping his steamed-up glasses and fixing them back on. 'All I'm doing is logging on and hoping that Mr Waymann's password comes on automatically, so that I can read his e-mails!'

'Whatever!' Daisy hissed. 'Just get a move on, that's all!'...

'Cool!' Winona said, moving forward to show the Waymanns and Jimmy the picture she'd just taken. 'Now I'd better take another one, just to make sure!'...

'Can you do it?' Daisy pestered. Every second was like a minute. Any time now the Waymanns would be coming back into the house...

'I'm into his inbox!' Nathan reported. He clicked the mouse and brought up Sent Items, which he clicked again. 'The last one was sent to jack.long@ashby city.com!'

Daisy took a deep breath. 'I knew it! What does it say?'...

'Is that the phone?' Mrs Waymann asked, reacting to a ringing sound from inside the house...

'The phone!' Nathan gasped. He jumped up, knocking
the laptop to the ground. 'I'm out of here!'

'Come back!' Daisy cried…

'I'm sorry, Winona, I have to go,' Mrs Waymann said. 'I
hope your picture comes out well. I shall be very
interested to see your article in the next edition of
Woodbridge Words.

With this, she flip-flopped hurriedly back into the
house…

Nathan made a quick getaway through the French
doors while Daisy scrambled to pick up the laptop. A
glance out into the hallway showed a blur of lime-
green and orange heading her way.

Cripes! Quick as a flash she darted through the
nearest door…

Mrs Waymann flip-
flopped into the lounge
and picked up the
phone. 'Hello?… Oh
hello there, Bernie… No,
that's quite all right, I'm
not busy … Yes, fire
away…'

Oh no! Daisy found herself in a tiny downstairs cloakroom. There was a loo, a washbasin and a towel hanging on a silver rail – and no way out!…

'Daisy Morelli?' Mrs Waymann asked, her face darkening as she spoke on the phone to the school caretaker. 'You say she's just been to your house and had a fight with Lennox? Something about his collar? Now slow down, Mr King, and explain to me one step at a time…'

No way out, except through a small window high up on the wall.

Daisy would have to climb up on to the loo and then on to the tank above. Then, if she stood on tiptoe, she could curl her fingers around the window frame and haul herself up towards the gap.

She was on the tank, trying not to disturb the can of air freshener, struggling to raise herself. *Ouch!* She slipped and put her foot on the can. *Hisssss!* Her bare, scratched legs were covered in lavender spray. The can rolled and fell on to the tiles…

'No, Mr King, I'm not questioning what you say. Nothing Daisy Morelli does ever surprises me. And you think I should consider barring her from the rest of the course at Highfield as a punishment? There's only one day to go, isn't there? Yes, I have little Jimmy Black round at my house this very minute…'

Please don't let Witchy Waymann hear me! Daisy pleaded.

She hauled herself up to the window a second time, and eased her way though. First her head and shoulders, then her belly. Now only her legs were dangling inside the cloakroom. But hey, it was a long drop to the ground outside…

'Just a minute, Mr King, I thought I heard something in the downstairs cloakroom.' Mrs Waymann put a hand over the phone and yelled for her husband. 'Mi-i-ichael! I can smell lavender! I heard a noise! Check the loo for me, would you?'

Mr Waymann said goodbye to Winona and Jimmy, then jogged into the house.

'Uh-oh!' Jimmy flinched.

'Let's go!' Wionona said…

Daisy wrigged her legs over the window ledge, swung for a moment like a monkey from the bars of a cage, then let herself drop on to the flower bed below.

Not roses this time, thank heavens. She landed in a patch of bedding plants, looked all round, then sprinted across the rows of lettuces to the hedge beyond…

'Nobody here!' Michael Waymann reported to his wife as he came into the lounge. 'But you're right, there's a strong smell of air freshener in there. Hmm, that's funny. Who knocked my laptop on to the floor? And I didn't think I'd left it turned on.'

'Stop wittering, Michael.' Crossly Mrs Waymann turned back to her conversation with the caretaker. 'Tell me, Bernie, have you any idea what Daisy could be up to?' …

'Phwoah, you stink!' Jimmy told Daisy, when the gang met up at the corner of Lilac Avenue.

'Of lavender!' Winona announced, turning up her nose.

'You owe me seven pounds fifty!' Nathan reminded Daisy.

'Yeah, thanks a lot, all of you!' Daisy muttered darkly. Everything had gone wrong and all they could talk about was stupid money and air freshener. She glowered at all three of them. 'There's only Mimi who's any good around here.

'*Rrrufff!*' Mimi yapped.

Daisy stormed off. 'You know what? I wish I'd never asked you to help in the first place!'

Seventeen

'Don't ask!' Daisy said when her dad wondered why she was giving off a strong whiff of old ladies.

'That smells like air freshener to me,' her clever mum guessed.

Daisy escaped her clutches and headed for the shower. 'Jimmy squirted me. We were messing around,' she fibbed.

Taking an extra shower was a big decision, but Daisy had to do it. She could stand mud and muck, but not the smell of lavender all over her.

Please don't let them ban me from Highfield! she prayed as the sharp pinpricks of hot water showered down.

I've only got one day left, and I've got to prove that Bernie is a spy! I've also got to find Robbie and stop him from signing for City! Deep in thought, she overdid the shower gel and ended up with mountains of white froth in the shower tray.

'Bedtime, Daisy!' her mum shouted from the bottom of the stairs.

So she waded through the foam, grabbed a big towel and made for her bedroom.

Phwoah, what's that flowery pong? Herbie asked.

Daisy tutted as she changed into her pyjamas. 'Bernie's trying to get me banned,' she told him. 'That means I won't be able to go back to Highfield ever again, or join the youth squad, or anything!'

What have you done this time? Herbie sighed. Daisy had made the mistake of leaving him behind earlier that evening. Now the hamster had got into his 'told you so!' mood.

'It wasn't my fault!' Daisy protested. 'I was only trying to prove that Bernie's spying for Ashby City!'

She was climbing into bed beside Herbie when her mum came to say goodnight.

'Good girl, you look lovely and clean,' Angie smiled, sitting on the edge of Daisy's bed. 'How's my star soccer player? Are you having a great week?'

'Yeah,' Daisy mumbled. Now was so *not* the time for

her mum to be nice. She felt tears well up and tried to bury her head in the pillow.

'Tired?' Angie asked, stroking Daisy's damp hair.

Daisy nodded and snuggled deeper under the duvet.

'I'm not surprised after all these fitness workouts,' her mum murmured. 'But you know, your dad and I are so proud of you... Daisy, you're not crying, are you?'

'Nope!' came the muffled answer.

Angie drew back the duvet. 'You are!' she said gently. 'Oh Daisy, what's wrong?'

She's in deep doo-doo again! Herbie squeaked.

Angie couldn't hear the hamster. 'Come on, love, tell me what's the matter.'

'Nothing!' Daisy sobbed. 'Well, if you want to know, I'm scared that Steelers will lose the match on Saturday and we won't be top of the league!' There, she said it. She'd confessed her worst fear!

Her mum smiled and tucked her in. 'Is that all?' she said softly. 'Don't worry, Daisy, your team will do OK. After all, they've got Robbie Exley-'

'Oh-oh-oh!' Daisy cried. 'That's just it – they haven't!' Where was Robbie? What had happened to him? Had he been kidnapped? Had Bernie tried to poison him?

'Well never mind.' Angie smoothed and patted the

duvet, then stood up and got ready to turn out the light. 'Try not to get upset, honey. After all, it's only a game.'

Wrong! Daisy thought as darkness fell. *This is more than a game. This is Steelers. This is Robbie. It's a case of life and death!*

'William King says he'll give us a lift into Highfield with Marc Predoux!' Jimmy announced next morning.

He'd arrived early at Daisy's place, before she'd finished breakfast.

'Hey, you look like something the cat dragged in,' he said, studying Daisy's pale, tired face and uncombed hair.

'Thanks,' Daisy muttered. She hadn't slept a wink for wondering whether or not they'd let her through the gates of Highfield.

'Come on!' Jimmy urged. 'William said to meet them at the corner of Woodbridge Road. It's our last day!'

Daisy was stiff. Her legs felt like lead, but she got her kit together, said goodbye to her mum, dad and goo-guck Mia, then set off behind Jimmy down the road.

What about me? a little voice called from the upstairs window.

Daisy looked up. 'Hang on, I forgot Herbie,' she muttered to Jimmy, scurrying back to collect him. She stuffed the hamster into the front pocket of her sports bag, then ran to catch up with Jimmy.

'Marc drives a big BMW,' Jimmy told Daisy. 'One of those four-wheel drives. William says he won't mind giving us a lift. He has to drive this way in any case. I saw William when I went to the paper shop with Dad. William's been staying with his uncle-'

'Stop!' Daisy groaned. Her head was whirling, but she caught this last scrap of information. 'Was William there at Bernie's house when…when, y'know… Lennox, the collar and all that?'

Jimmy nodded. 'He was watching through the window. He said Bernie was well mad.'

'Uhhh!' Daisy groaned. Suddenly she didn't fancy the lift with Marc Predoux in his big BMW.

'Don't worry, William thought it was a laugh,' Jimmy assured her. 'He just says you're nuts, that's all.'

'Thanks.' Daisy didn't smile, but went on earnestly, 'Jimmy, if they ban me, it'll be up to you to carry on spying. We haven't got enough proof against Bernie yet. I mean, there's the e-mail to Jack Long on Mr Waymann's computer, but Nathan and me never had the chance to read it. It's not enough. We need more, and it'll be down to you to get it.'

'Yeah, yeah,' Jimmy muttered. 'Listen, I think Robbie will show up today, and everything will be cool.'

Daisy frowned. 'What if he doesn't? What if Bernie really has drugged him and is trying to brainwash him into leaving Steelers and signing for Ashby City – what then?'

There was no time for Jimmy to answer as he spotted Marc's car pulling up to the kerb. A door opened, inviting Daisy and Jimmy to hop into the gleaming silver monster.

'Hi there,' William greeted them, giving Jimmy a special little grin. 'How are your legs?' he asked Daisy.

'What's wrong with my legs?' she blushed, glancing down at them.

Marc signalled and rejoined the flow of traffic.

'I bet you were picking thorns out of them all last night,' William teased.

Daisy didn't laugh. 'Never mind my legs, how's Robbie?' she asked Marc with a meaningful look towards Jimmy. 'Is he gonna show up for training today?'

Their superstar driver swung into City Road. 'Don't know,' he admitted. 'I heard Kevin was pretty upset about him missing yesterday's session though. He said no one skipped training without a good reason, and if Robbie thought he was bigger than the club, he had another think coming.'

'Wow!' Jimmy gasped.

'See!' Daisy grunted. 'Remember, Jim, if they don't let me in, you have to take over!'

By now they were turning into the players' car park at Highfield and the players' chat turned towards the next day's match.

'I hear Jack Long has got something special up his sleeve,' William told Marc.

'Who told you that?' the Steelers' star defender asked.

'My Uncle Bernie mentioned it,' William replied.

Daisy tuned into the conversation with every nerve ending in her body. Master spy Bernie had been giving William the lowdown on Ashby City. 'What did I tell you?' she hissed at Jimmy.

'Jack's tactics are dead secret, but Uncle Bernie reckons we'd better watch out,' William went on.

Marc parked his BMW. 'Yeah, well you tell your uncle we don't scare easily.'

Jimmy and Daisy hopped out of the car and followed William and Marc through the players' door.

'Listen!' Daisy pulled Jimmy to one side. 'This is really, really serious! Bernie means business. In fact, he's probably already got Robbie to sign for City. I wouldn't be surprised if Robbie runs out in City strip tomorrow afternoon and scores three goals against us!'

'Whoah!' Jimmy protested.

'We have to tell Kevin!' Daisy decided. 'No more messing about with this spying stuff. If we don't see Kevin today, it'll be too late!'

'No, I mean whoah, look over there!' Jimmy insisted. He pointed to the door of the changing room.

Daisy had been too worked up to notice Mrs Waymann waiting by the door. 'Uhhh!' she sighed, feeling as if a football had just whacked her in the stomach.

'Ah, Daisy!' Mrs Waymann said in her loud, head teacher voice. 'I need to have a little word!'

'You thought you had outsmarted me!' the Wicked Witch of the West shrieked at Daisy. Her face was green, her fingernails long and sharp. 'But I have been watching you, you little fool! Now you will never follow the yellow brick road and find your dream!'

'B-b-but!' Daisy cried. 'This is the land that I dreamed of! This is way up high – somewhere over the rainbow. I want to stay here with Scarecrow, Lion and Tinman. We're off to meet the Wizard of Oz!'

'And I say you will never find happiness!' The Wicked Witch darted at Daisy to snatch back her sparkling red shoes. 'Give them to me, you wretch!'

'Run, Daisy!' Scarecrow cried, tripping over his straw feet.

'Run!' Tinman echoed, his joints creaking as he fled.

But Lion found his courage and stood his ground. 'I will save you, Daisy!' he roared.

'Get out of my way!' the Witch shrieked, sweeping Lion aside with her broomstick. Thunderclouds gathered over her head and lightning split the dark sky. The Witch's eyes burned into Daisy, who quivered from head to foot.

'I will never give in!' Daisy swore.

Thunder cracked as the Witch took hold of Daisy's wrist. 'The shoes – give them to me!'

'Daisy, Mr King has told me some very serious news about you,' Mrs Waymann began, taking Daisy by the arm and drawing her to one side.

'It's not true!' Daisy protested, unable to get the Witch's green face out of her mind. It didn't help that Waymann was wearing her dazzling green top, plus bright red nail varnish.

'How do you know it's not true before I tell you what it is?' Waymann asked.

'If it's about last night, we were only trying to-'

'Stop! Before you go any further, I want to tell you how disappointed I am in you, Daisy Morelli.'

'Why, what have I done?' Daisy squirmed as Darren and a couple of other kids strolled by. This was it – Waymann was going to deliver the killer blow and tell Daisy she was banned from Highfield. She would have to hang up her boots forever.

The end of a brilliant career! Daisy groaned to herself. All her dreams of lifting the FA Cup above her head to the roar of a hundred thousand fans shattered in an instant.

'It seems you went to Mr King's house and attacked his dog.' Mrs Waymann's frown was puzzled. 'Even for you, Daisy, that was a very strange thing to do.'

Oh no! Daisy sighed to herself. *What will Mum and Dad say? They're gonna be mega ashamed! They'll ground me for five years at least!*

'You stole Lennox's collar,' Waymann went on. 'Mr King really is very angry with you, Daisy.'

'But he's trying to make us lose the premiership!' Daisy began. She paused, then, with nothing to lose, she rushed on. 'Bernie's kidnapped Robbie Exley, then drugged and brainwashed him. Now he's getting him to sign for Ashby City!'

Mrs Waymann slowly raised her eyebrows. 'Sometimes, Daisy Morelli, I wonder what planet you're living on.'

'B-b-but!'

'No buts. I want you to listen carefully. I came here this morning with Michael – Mr Waymann – with only one thing in mind, and that was to ban you from this soccer school.'

'Oh no!' Daisy groaned. 'I'll leave Lennox alone from now on, I promise!'

'Be quiet, Daisy!' Waymann barked. 'I haven't finished. Then Michael discussed the problem with me and he pointed out that getting you banned from Highfield would only bring bad publicity to Woodbridge Road Juniors.

'Picture the headlines – "Woodbridge Pupil Given the Red Card! Local school admits it was a major mistake to send their worst pupil to Kevin Crowe's Soccer Academy".'

Daisy sighed and hung her head. She longed to be with Jimmy, Darren and the others, fastening up their boots, ready to rush out on to the pitch for their final day's training.

'So-ooh,' Mrs Waymann concluded slowly, 'I have decided, Daisy – in spite of everything, and directly against what Mr King wishes me to do – to let you finish the course.'

'Wrrroaghhh!' Lion roared.

Tinman sobbed for joy. Scarecrow grinned from ear to ear.

'Take courage!' Lion proclaimed. 'We have vanquished the Wicked Witch of the West!'

Eighteen

'...provided you don't put another foot wrong!' the head teacher said, staring deep into Daisy's eyes. 'No more nonsense, no more strange goings-on – understand?'

'Yes!' Daisy gasped. *Wow, thank you mousy Michael! Thanks for believing in me!*

'But!' Waymann held up her forefinger in dire warning. 'If you let me down, Daisy, your life won't be worth living.'

'Yes, miss. No, miss. Thanks, miss!'

Daisy's head whirled. She must be going mad, because she could have sworn she'd just had a glimpse of Nathan Moss going into Kevin Crowe's office. *No way! That's totally nuts!*

'Go!' Mrs Waymann ordered.

Daisy shot off into the empty changing room. Twenty seconds later she was back out in the corridor in her kit, ready to race outside.

Now I am going crazy! she thought. There was not only Nathan, but Winona in the manager's room. Yes – that was the back of Winona's curly-wurly hair, all tied up in a pink velvet scrunchy and hanging down her back like My Little Pony. Nathan was on her left side, and to her right was Karl Andrews, the sports reporter for the *Helston Herald*.

'Winona and Nathan are cub reporters,' Karl was telling Kevin as Daisy crept nearer. 'They contacted me early this morning to say they're working on *Woodbridge Words*, the school magazine for Woodbridge Road Junior School. Winona would like to do an interview with Robbie Exley. I said I'd help get her through the doors. They both seem like nice, clever kids.'

'Sorry, no can do,' the Steelers' manager answered with a frown.

You can say that again! Daisy thought. *How can you interview an invisible superstar?* But then Winona and Nathan had known that and had still wormed their way in. The interview was only an excuse. Talk about clever – they were total geniuses!

'Robbie isn't available for interview,' Kevin told the cub reporters.

'Hm,' Karl cut in. He was like a bloodhound picking up a scent. 'What about this rumour we picked up yesterday that there's a transfer deal in the offing?'

'No comment,' Kevin grunted, standing up and showing them to the door.

Daisy stood rooted to the spot.

'Tell you what – these two can go and watch the Academy kids and write a report on that,' the manager suggested more kindly. 'But as for you, Karl, I'd be grateful if you'd go right back to your office and file a report saying "No Transfer Deal for Robbie", OK?'

The reporter shrugged. 'I hear he didn't show up for training yesterday. Is that true?'

Kevin Crowe was used to dealing with the press. He turned the question round and asked, 'Who told you that?'

'We picked it up from a website. It turned out to be a reliable source,' Karl said.

Yeah, Bernie King! It was time for Daisy to step out and show herself. This was her big chance. So she took a deep breath and knocked on the open door.

'Daisy!' Winona met her face to face. She smiled and sounded glad, but her eyes were flashing. 'Don't say anything!' she muttered in a low voice without moving her lips.

Daisy paused. 'Get out of my way, Winona!' she muttered back.

'Don't say a word!' My Little Pony mouthed. 'Let me and Nathan snoop around first!'

'But you never told me you were gonna do this!' Daisy protested, as Karl and Kevin shook hands and said goodbye.

'No time!' Winona explained. She pushed Daisy backwards down the corridor, then said in an extra-loud voice, 'Daisy, shouldn't you be outside with the others?'

Kevin glanced at his watch. 'Yeah, you'd better

scoot,' he agreed. 'And Karl, read my lips – no transfer deal, got it!'

'You're so dead!' Daisy whispered to Winona, while Nathan frowned and tapped the side of his nose. 'And you, Nathan!' Daisy added.

'Leave it to us!' Winona insisted, pushing Daisy on her way. 'Give us a couple of hours and we'll get you all the proof you need!'

'Loosen up, Daisy!' Gary shouted from the touchline. 'Get in there and tackle! That's more like it!' It was hard to concentrate on the ball with all this other stuff going on, but Daisy tried. This was their last training session, the end of what should have been a magic week.

'Nice one, Jimmy!' Gary called, as Jimmy received the pass from Daisy and headed the ball into the net.

Jimmy gave a victory leap before the others piled on top of him and only his skinny legs poked out from under the heap of bodies.

As the teams lined up for a centre kick, Daisy had time to clock Winona and Nathan, the super-sleuths, interviewing everything that moved.

'Excuse me, Mr Crowe, can you give us a preview of tomorrow's line-up for the game against City?' Winona asked, pencil poised over her glittery notepad.

'I told you, I'm busy,' the manager snapped, gathering his first-team squad for a tactical talk.

No Robbie! Daisy noticed, as Gary blew the whistle.

'Marc, what are Steelers' chances of winning the Premiership?' Nathan darted into the midst of Kevin's team while the manager dealt with Winona.

'Scoot!' Marc told him with a grin.

Yeah, no wonder Bernie's standing there smiling! Daisy thought darkly.

The master spy's plot was working. He was standing by the dugout looking dead pleased with himself.

'Daisy, I want you in goal,' Gary decided, sending her to the end closest to Kevin and his team.

'Mr Waymann, will you be refereeing the match tomorrow?' Winona grabbed her chance to interview the Head's husband.

Michael Waymann shook his head. 'What are you doing here?' he asked.

'Writing an article for *Woodbridge Words*,' Winona assured him. 'Nathan's the photographer this time. I'm the reporter.'

Click-click. Nathan took action shots of the first

team beginning their training.

'Mr Waymann, is it true that Robbie Exley has been left out of the team?' Winona asked in her most innocent voice. 'What can you tell us about the report on the website that Robbie is about to sign for Ashby City?'

The goalmouth seemed wider than the Grand Canyon. Darren Longlegs powered down the pitch towards Daisy. This would have to be the save of a lifetime…

Winona built up towards her killer question, noticing that the school caretaker had spotted her and Nathan and was making his way along the touchline.

'Tell me, Mr Waymann,' she said hurriedly, 'did you know that Bernie King was once a groundsman at Ashby City? And what would you think of the idea that he might be here as a spy for Steelers' arch rivals?'

Darren blasted a shot at goal.

Daisy guessed which way the ball was going and dived full length for a spectacular save.

Oof! She landed on her shoulder, with the ball clutched to her stomach.

Mousy Waymann gave Winona the brush-off. 'Don't be silly,' he said. 'You've been watching too many James Bond movies.'

'What do these kids want?' Bernie said angrily as he

'He denied everything!' Winona told Daisy as the

'He totally lost it,' Nathan reported, remembering
how the school caretaker had heard the accusations,
then turned purple, stamped and stormed.

'Which only proves he's guilty,' Daisy pointed out.
'If he was innocent, he'd have laughed it off.'

'Wow, Daisy!' Winona was impressed. 'When you
grow up you'll have to be a psych-i-ol-i-thing-ummy!'

'Psychiatrist,' Nathan said.

'No thanks, I'm gonna play for England.' Daisy had
bigger things in mind. 'But listen, we've got a
problem.'

'Which is?' Winona wanted to know.

'That Bernie knows we know!' Daisy announced.
It was the shoot-out at the OK Corral.

*Sheriff Morelli watched the sun rise in the sky. At high
noon, she would strap on her six-shooter and face King
Bernie, man to man.*

*'Don't do it, Daisy!' Jimmy the Kid implored. 'Bernie's
the fastest draw in the West!'*

*'A girl's gotta do what a girl's gotta do!' she drawled.
'And there ain't room for both Bernie and me in this here
town!'*

The sun reached its peak. Morelli pulled the brim of her Stetson low down on her forehead. There was not a breath of wind as she strode down Main Street.

The King watched her come. He was unshaven and dressed in black, hands poised over his holster. 'Get ready to die, Morelli!' he sneered.

The sheriff didn't flinch as she stood face to face with the outlaw. A sudden gust of wind blew a ball of tumbleweed across the dusty street. She waited until big bad Bernie went for his gun.

Kerpow! *A single gunshot broke the silence. The King was dead.*

'Yeah, sorry, Daisy,' Winona said. 'I thought I could get Mr Waymann to confess, then we could go to Kevin Crowe with the proof.'

'Nice try,' Nathan said.

Winona blushed and batted her eyelashes.

'Nice try – nothing!' Daisy disagreed. Didn't Winona know anything about spying? Didn't she realise that you never blew your cover and came out into the open?

'OK, kids, gather round!' Gary interrupted the heated discussion. 'We've got an early finish today because Kevin needs me to train the first team this afternoon.'

A groan went up from the soccer pupils.

'But!' Gary went on. 'The good news is that I've got a fistful of tickets here for the match tomorrow. You can bring your families and sit in the directors' box. How about that?'

'Cool!' they cried.

'And before we finish here, I want to announce the three names who will be joining the junior squad, plus my own star player of the week!'

'That's you, Daisy!' Jimmy predicted, sidling to the back of the group. 'You already know you're joining the Juniors.'

Daisy joined her mate. 'It might be you,' she insisted.

But Jimmy shook his head, not daring to hope.

'Wouldn't it be cool though – you and me, Jimmy – coming to Highfield, training with the Juniors together…!'

'I've discussed this with Kevin,' Gary went on. 'And Daisy, we'd like you to come back and train with us.'

'Good on you, Daisy! Cool! Nice one!' the other kids said.

Daisy blinked and scuffled her feet on the turf. Mega embarrassment, but wow!

'And the second person is…' Gary paused.

Daisy felt Jimmy hold his breath. She crossed her fingers for him.

'…Darren!' Gary said.

'Yeah!' Everyone clapped. Darren was well liked, and he was a great player.

Jimmy's head dropped. 'I knew it wouldn't be me,' he sighed.

'It still could be.' *Please, please, please!* Daisy prayed.

'And the third person is the one I've also picked as star player of the week. This kid has put in one hundred and fifty per cent effort, plus he's a natural ball player,' Gary announced. He looked at each pupil, smiled and passed them over until his gaze reached the back of the group. 'That's you, Jimmy. Without a shadow of a doubt, you've been the best of a very talented bunch!'

'You should've seen him!' Daisy told Herbie after the excitement was over.

While the others ate their sandwiches, she'd taken the hamster out of her locker and brought him up to date with events. 'You know Jimmy – footie is his life. So when Gary said his name, it was like he'd won a million pounds!'

Jimmy's cool, Herbie agreed.

'He never thought it would be him, but that's Jimmy for you – so *not* bigheaded!'

I like him, the hamster agreed. *Let's have a party.*

Daisy gazed out over the green turf of Highfield. The week had been better than she could ever have dreamed. She ought to be totally happy, but instead she let out a sigh.

It's this Bernie King thing, isn't it? Herbie asked quietly.

Since Winona's face-off with Bernie, Daisy hadn't caught sight of the enemy. She had no idea what he planned to do next. 'Yeah,' she sighed, 'it's the King thing.'

You've reached a dead end? You don't know what to do?

'Right.'

Bernie might still be able to get you banned from Highfield.

'Yeah, I hadn't thought of that.'

It's possible. And on top of that, he's still got Robbie Exley kidnapped and drugged up to the eyeballs.

'Yeah, thanks, Herbie!' Thanks for reminding her!

You've only got this afternoon to nail Bernie and save Steelers' skin. Herbie laid it on the line for Daisy.

'Yeah, and Winona didn't help!' she frowned.

Forget that. What's your next move?

'You tell me.' Walking slowly out to the touchline, Daisy stared up at the main stand with its rows of empty seats. She felt the chill wind of defeat.

Use Winona to worm your way into Low Moor this afternoon, Herbie suggested. *Let her do her cub reporter thing again. Everyone believes she's the real thing. She can interview Jack Long about tomorrow's match, and while she keeps him busy, you and Jimmy can search the place for clues about Robbie!*

'It's too risky,' Nathan said when Daisy outlined the plan.

'Yeah, Bernie's probably already told them we're spies,' Winona agreed.

'You're just chicken!' Daisy scoffed. 'Come on, Jimmy, we'll have to do it by ourselves!'

Winona followed her out of the changing room. 'How will you get in without me and Nathan?' she challenged.

'Hire a helicopter to drop us on to the pitch.

Parachute in. Dig a tunnel,' Agent 0077 grunted. 'Ha-ha!'

'Daisy's right – we have to do something to get Robbie back,' Jimmy said, dragging Nathan into the corridor. 'Which bus do we get to Low Moor?'

'The number thirty-two,' the expert told him. Nathan knew every route in the city. 'A bus leaves from City Road every twenty minutes, but I still say it's way too risky.'

'Me too.' Winona didn't know much about football, but even she had heard of Ashby City and their fierce manager, Jack Long.

'Give me a better idea,' Daisy muttered, striding ahead. She had Herbie neatly zipped up in the front pocket of her rucksack. Nothing would stop her now.

'Yeah, Nathan, think of something!' Winona said.

'Mega risky!' Nathan repeated, unable to come up with another plan.

He and Winona watched Jimmy team up with Daisy and leave Highfield. Winona looked at Nathan. Nathan looked at Winona.

'They're pretty brave,' Winona admitted.

'Yeah, or really, really stupid,' Nathan said.

They watched Daisy and Jimmy cross the car park. 'What shall we do?' Winona asked.

Nathan frowned. Maybe it was the bus ride across the city that swayed him in the end. 'Daisy, Jimmy –

wait for us!' he called, breaking into a run.

Daisy grinned as a number thirty-two pulled in at the stop. 'Hurry up!' she cried. 'Four tickets to Low Moor,' she told the driver, as Jimmy, Nathan and Winona plonked themselves down on the back seat of the bus.

Nineteen

'The wheels on the bus go round and round!' Jimmy belted out his old playschool song. 'Round and round, round and round…'

'Back off, Jimmy!' Daisy groaned. How could she take the Robbie kidnap seriously while her best mate was acting like a three-year-old?

'The spies on the bus go creep, creep, creep…'

'Jimmy!' Winona tutted. She looked round uneasily. 'Someone might hear.'

'Creep, creep, creep…'

Nathan ignored Jimmy's high spirits. 'If this plan of

yours goes pear-shaped, don't blame me,' he warned Daisy.

But Daisy stroked Herbie on his bald patch and looked straight ahead. 'It won't go wrong,' she insisted.

'Well, we'll soon find out.' Nathan told them that this was their stop.

The four of them rolled and staggered down the aisle, waited for the hiss of the opening door, then jumped off the bus. Looming over them, beyond a wide pavement, was the shiny new stadium of Ashby City.

'We're nuts!' Nathan said, staring up at the City sign above the main entrance. He shook his head, dragged his feet, looked like he was about to do a runner.

Winona turned to wait. 'Buck up, Nathan!' she said in her best PE teacher voice. 'This is really exciting. We don't want to miss any of it, do we?'

Pulling himself together, Nathan followed meekly.

'I'm Winona Jones, and this is Jimmy Black, Daisy Morelli and Nathan Moss!' Winona told the man on the Reception desk of the rival club. 'We're from Woodbridge Road Junior School.'
Daisy clenched her teeth and muttered, 'Watch it, Winona. Don't sound too in-your-face!'

'We're writing an article on the Premiership battle

for *Woodbridge Words*,' Winona went on boldly. 'We'd like an interview with Jack Long, please!'

'You and a hundred others,' the young guy said, as if he couldn't care less. He carried on tapping at the keyboard of his computer.

'Hmm.' Winona frowned. 'But we have an appointment at two o'clock. Karl Andrews from the *Helston Herald* phoned Mr Long and fixed it for us!'

Wow! Daisy and Jimmy exchanged admiring looks. Winona was definitely good!

Tap-tap-tap. Reception Man worked on.

'We've already had an interview with Kevin Crowe,' Winona explained, taking out her sparkly pink notepad. 'These are the notes I took for the article.'

'Yeah, yeah, whatever.' *Tap-tap-tappety-tap*. 'Go ahead, but watch Mr Long doesn't bite your head off. He wasn't in the best of moods last time I saw him.'

'Thanks!' Winona said, zooming past the desk with the other three in tow.

'Right, this is where we have to split up!' Daisy instructed.

The Low Moor offices ran down a long corridor, just like Highfield. But here the carpets were bright red, not blue, and all the pictures on the walls were of famous City players from the eighties and nineties.

'This feels weird!' Jimmy said with a shiver.

'We'll find the players' changing rooms and start looking for Robbie,' Daisy went on. 'Winona, you take Nathan and con your way into Jack Long's room. See what you can find out from the man at the top.'

Winona nodded briskly. 'Ready, Nathan? Have you got the camera? Let's go!'

'What are we hoping to find exactly?' Jimmy asked as Daisy crept ahead down the corridor.

'Ssh!' she warned, pressing herself flat against the wall and making Jimmy do the same. 'I thought I heard footsteps!'

No one came, though there were voices in the distance, and then laughter. After a while, the two spies carried on.

'We need to find Robbie, or at the very least, some proof that he's been here,' Daisy explained.

If her kidnap theory was right, Bernie King had slipped something nasty into their star player's drink, carted him away and brainwashed him until he'd agreed to sign for City. But that must have been nearly two days ago, and by now, Robbie should be back on his feet and trapped in a new contract with Steelers' rivals. 'I expect Jack Long is the brains behind it,' she told Jimmy. 'He'll do anything it takes to make sure City win the Premiership!'

'Excuse me, Mr Long?' Winona had knocked on the door marked *Manager* then opened it.

A man with a long nose and thin face looked up from his desk. 'Who wants to know?' he grunted.

'I'm Winona Jones!' Winona said brightly. 'And this is Nathan Moss. We're from Woodbridge Road Junior School.'

'Look, there are the changing rooms!' Jimmy dragged Daisy to the left, then took shelter behind a row of metal lockers. They ducked down low as two men in red tracksuits walked by.

'Take cover!' Corporal Black dodged the bullets and made it to the muddy trench. Sergeant Morelli was close on his heels, crawling on her belly then rolling to safety.

Ack-ack-ack! A German machine gunner in the enemy trench aimed and fired. The bullets thudded into the earth.

'Made it!' Morelli sighed. When the shooting stopped she raised her head above ground and peered out at a wasteland of barbed wire and mud. 'We're the only two left alive!' she told the corporal. 'It's up to us now, Jim!'

Daisy waited until the coast was clear. She checked her watch. It was almost two o'clock. 'Let's hope the squad is out training,' she whispered.

'Duck!' Jimmy warned again.

This time the heavy footsteps sounded familiar, and then the loud huffing and puffing of a wheezy animal.

'*Hugh-hugh-huff!*' Fat Lennox waddled along the Low Moor corridor. There was no mistaking his slobbery chops and broad, steel-studded collar.

Daisy gasped. Her eyes nearly started out of her head.

'Here, boy!' Bernie King grunted as his dog stopped to sniff around the lockers.

'Go away, Lennox!' Daisy breathed, eyeball to bloodshot eyeball with the enemy.

'*Sniff-snuffle-slobber.*' Lennox recognised her and let out a low growl.

'Come here, Lennox!' Bernie insisted, ready to turn into one of the changing rooms.

'*Grrrr!*' The dog waddled up to Jimmy and took a sniff.

Quickly Jimmy took a half-sucked Polo mint from his pocket, let the dog smell it, then silently rolled it down the corridor. Fat Lennox heaved himself around and waddled after the mint. *Wumph!* He snaffled it between his droopy jaws.

'Here, boy!' Bernie repeated grumpily. And this time the bulldog obeyed.

Good thinking! Herbie squeaked at Jimmy, as Bernie and Fat Lennox turned into the changing room and disappeared inside.

'Phew!' Daisy breathed again. 'But listen, that was Bernie – right here at Low Moor, acting like he owns the place!'

'Yeah!' Jimmy nodded.

'You know what this means?' Daisy hissed, looking right and left, but staying well hidden.

'Yeah!' Jimmy nodded.

Daisy crouched low and got into a huddle with her best mate. 'I don't like to boast, Jimmy, but it means I was right!'

No way was Jack Long as nice as Kevin Crowe, Winona decided.

For a start, he had a mean look. There was that long nose, and he had small eyes that were too close together. Then there was the way he talked.

'I don't care if Karl Andrews sent you to get an interview. I wouldn't care if the Prime Minister himself had sent you, I don't want to waste my time talking to a couple of stupid kids, OK!'

Winona frowned and dug in her heels. 'Kevin Crowe gave us a really long interview,' she pointed out.

'Yeah, yeah, Mr Nice Guy! Well, guess what, I'm not Kevin Crowe and you two are a waste of space. Now get out!'

'Perhaps just a photo then?' Winona suggested, dragging Nathan into the room. 'You carry on with what you're doing and act naturally. No need to take any notice of the camera.'

Jack Long stood up. He was over six feet tall. 'Don't you understand English?' he muttered. 'What part of "get out!" don't you understand?'

In less than a minute, before Daisy and Jimmy had moved from their hiding place behind the lockers, Bernie King came out of the changing room alone. He closed the door and walked off.

'Where's Lennox?' Jimmy whispered.

'He must have left him in there,' Daisy decided. 'Let's go and see.'

'What if he barks?' Jimmy asked.

'We'll have to risk it,' Daisy decided. She needed to know what Bernie had been doing in that room. Had he got poor Robbie tied up and hidden away in a shower cubicle? And was Lennox standing guard?

Slowly Daisy led the way to the door. Jimmy

checked up and down the empty corridor. 'Hurry up, let's get this over with!' he hissed.

Daisy tried the handle. It turned. She opened the door.

'Quick!' Jimmy cried. A tall man in a suit had appeared at the far end of the corridor.

Daisy and Jimmy slipped inside the changing room. It was dark, with only one small window high on the far wall. Gradually they were able to see that there was a row of shower cubicles down one side, more lockers down the other, and rows of benches running across the room.

'*Grrrrrrr!*' Lennox growled.

Daisy and Jimmy felt as if they were treading on eggshells as they made for the showers.

'I'm personally showing you to the door!' Jack Long told Winona and Nathan as he strode past the changing rooms. 'But only because I want to sack the guy on Reception who let you in!'

'Don't do that!' Winona gasped. 'It wasn't his fault.'

Nathan kept quiet. *I knew this was too risky*, he said to himself. *What am I doing here? I must be nuts!*

'Out!' Jack Long yelled, pointing across Reception to the revolving door.

Winona took a deep breath. After all, she was in so

deep, it couldn't really get any worse. 'Just one last question, Mr Long,' she said chirpily. 'Is there any truth in the rumour that you've signed a new contract with Robbie Exley?'

'*Grrrr!*' Lennox growled. He sat on a bench beside an untidy pile of clothes.

Daisy and Jimmy tiptoed past him.

'Robbie's here somewhere – I know he is!' Daisy whispered.

'Wow, Daisy, this is doing my head in!' Jimmy groaned. 'The dog might pounce at any second, or Bernie might come back.'

'Not here!' Daisy muttered, looking inside the first shower. Nothing in the second, or the third, and right down to the end of the row. 'Hmm,' she frowned.

'*Hhrrrugh!*' Lennox coughed.

'Look under the benches, Jimmy.' Daisy grew desperate. 'We need a clue – something – anything!'

They dropped to their hands and knees and searched the floor, knocking trainers off the bench and dragging sweatshirts down on top of them.

'*Aawwgh!*' Lennox opened his mouth and yawned. Then he sniffed at Jimmy's pocket for more Polos.

'Ouch!' Daisy yelped as she raised her head too suddenly and knocked it on the bench.

A pair of football boots fell down beside her.

'Oh!' Daisy gasped, picking the boots up. 'Oh, Jimmy, oh!'

'What's up?' he hissed, dreading footsteps and the turn of the door handle.

'Look at these!' she whimpered. The boots were soft, white leather with narrow blue stripes down the side.

'What about them?' Jimmy asked.

Daisy turned the boots this way and that. 'They're special. There's only one person who wears this style,' she explained, her voice breaking with excitement. 'You know who that is!'

Jimmy got it at last. 'Robbie!' he gasped.

Daisy nodded.

The door handle turned and Bernie King walked in. But it didn't matter any more. Daisy had the boots. She held them close to her chest and ran like a rugby player scoring a try.

Bernie blocked the doorway. He put out his hands to stop Daisy.

She flew at the caretaker, made contact and knocked him sideways. 'Here, Jimmy, catch!' she yelled, passing the boots as she sprawled in a heap.

Jimmy caught and ran. He leaped clean over Bernie and Daisy, then pelted down the corridor with the boots.

Daisy scrambled to her feet. 'Try talking your way

out of this!' she yelled at Bernie King.

'Stop! Come back!' the caretaker spluttered. But Daisy and Jimmy were gone.

Lennox sat on the bench and yawned.

'Call yourself a guard dog, you stupid mutt!' Bernie King ranted. He watched helplessly as Daisy and Jimmy vanished through the revolving doors.

Twenty

'I'll tell you something, Gary – I never want another week like this one!' The Steelers manager sat at his desk, staring out of the window across the huge Highfield car park.

'Don't tell me!' his assistant agreed. He handed Kevin a cup of coffee and sat in a chair by the window.

'It's put years on me!' the boss sighed. 'And that's before we even get to the match!'

'Yeah well, Robbie doing his vanishing trick didn't help,' Gary pointed out, easing his feet up on to a low table. 'Then there's been a couple of injury problems, plus all that transfer rubbish flying about in the press.'

'Never again!' Kevin groaned, standing up to stretch. 'But if we win tomorrow, I guess it will all have been worth it.'

There was silence as the two men sipped their coffees – silence broken by a kerfuffle out in the car park.

'What's that racket?' Kevin asked, striding to the window.

Bernie King screeched to a halt on the gravel. He'd raced across town in his silver hatchback, overtaking the number thirty-two bus on the way.

'That's Bernie's car!' Nathan had gasped, looking down from the top deck.

'Oh dash it!' Winona had cried. 'Now he'll get to Highfield before us!'

But the caretaker had been held up in rush hour traffic and he'd only just made it into the car park before Winona and Nathan hopped off the bus.

'There he is!' Winona cried, as Bernie slammed the door of his car. 'Come on, Nathan, we've got to stop him!'

'Why? What for? I don't see the point.' Nathan huffed and puffed as Winona sprinted towards the players' entrance.

'He's gonna get to Kevin and poison his mind against Daisy!' Winona cried.

Bernie let Lennox out of the passenger seat. 'Go fetch!' he told the dog, pointing at Nathan and Winona.

'I'm out of here!' Nathan whimpered, making a swift left out of the building.

'What a geek!' Winona muttered, falling out of love with Nathan, then ploughing straight on towards Kevin's office.

'*Hrugh-huff-hrugh!*' Lennox trundled after Nathan.

'Not him! Get the girl!' Bernie yelled. He caught up with Fat Lennox and dragged him down the corridor.

Just then, Kevin's door opened and the manager came out. 'What's going on?' he demanded.

'Mr Crowe, I need to talk to you!' Winona cried. Her hair had fallen out of its scrunchy, she was panting for breath as fat Lennox caught up with her and pinned her against the wall.

'It's nothing,' Bernie tried to tell Kevin. He stuck up his arms like a traffic cop. 'Everything's under control.'

The Steelers manager was joined at his door by his assistant. 'Isn't that the kid who wanted to write an article for her school magazine?' Gary asked.

'Please, I need to talk!' Winona begged, feeling Lennox's breath on her legs.

'Take no notice!' Bernie cut in. 'Come along, young lady. Kevin's busy. He doesn't want you bothering him again.'

'B-b-but!' Winona protested.

Kevin Crowe sighed. It had been a long week. 'Yeah, get her out of here,' he told Bernie wearily, turning and firmly closing his door.

'Hey, there's Winona in Bernie King's car!' Jimmy gasped.

He and Daisy had been on the next bus. They'd made it to Highfield in record time.

'Help!' Winona hammered on the car window. 'Help, I'm being kidnapped!'

It was impossible to make out what she was saying.

'It looks like Bernie beat us to it!' Daisy muttered. 'He got to Kevin before us.'

'Yeah, but we've got Robbie's boots,' Jimmy reminded her, ducking down with Daisy behind a parked car to make sure that Bernie didn't see them.

Daisy clutched the evidence. 'You're right!' she nodded, easing her way between two cars.

A movement from inside one of the cars made her look up.

She glanced up again, then froze.

The woman in the driver's seat glared down at her, and wound down her window.

'Daisy Dis-aster Morelli!' Mrs Waymann cried. 'I don't know what you're up to, but it's definitely no good!'

The Head had pounced before Jimmy and Daisy had time to scarper. She marched them into Highfield, one-two, one-two.

Oh no! This can't be happening! Tell me it's a bad dream! Daisy moaned to herself.

'Michael!' Witchy Waymann spied her husband at work in the room with the computers. 'Can you stop what you're doing and come and help me with these two scallywags?'

So near and yet so far! Daisy groaned.

'What's up?' Mousy Michael asked.

'Don't ask, Michael, don't ask!' Mrs Waymann had been in the car park waiting for her husband to finish work when she'd spotted Daisy and Jimmy creeping around.

'We were only playing hide and seek!' Daisy squeaked.

'Yeah, hide and seek!' Jimmy nodded.

'Quiet!' Waymann snapped. 'I don't believe a word you say.'

'Erm…' Mr Waymann began.

'Erm, what?' his wife demanded. 'Come on, Michael, spit it out!'

'Erm, don't you think you're being a teeny bit hard?'

'No I don't! What I think is that Daisy is up to no

good, and Jimmy's got dragged in as usual.' Mrs Waymann showed no mercy. 'This time I'm not going to listen to you, Michael. I plan to take them home in my car and make sure nothing embarrassing happens!'

Oh no! Daisy sighed. Waymann didn't realise what she was doing. Now nothing could stop the triumphant march of Jack Long and Ashby City!

Agent 0077 knew that her number was up.

She'd come through a lot and served her country well. But the forces of evil in the world were too strong.

'This is it,' she murmured, holding her head up and expecting the worst. 'Shoot me now, get it over with.'

Waymann flashed her an evil smile. The diamond set into her front tooth glinted. 'You're clever, Agent Morelli, but not clever enough.'

0077 gave a defiant shrug. 'You may win the battle, Waymann, but you'll never win the war!'

The enemy spymaster raised her gold-plated revolver and pressed it against Morelli's head…

'Hey there, Daisy. Hey, Jimmy!' Kevin and Gary said as they came out of the office and spotted two of their stars of the future.

Yes! Daisy sprang forward, free of Waymann's clutches. *This is it! This is the biggest, most important moment of my life!*

'Anyone want a lift home?' Gary offered, taking out his car keys.

'It's OK, I'll take them,' Mrs Waymann stepped in quickly.

Daisy took a deep, deep breath, then held up Robbie's soft, supple white leather boots. 'Robbie Exley's been kidnapped!' she announced in a loud, clear voice. 'These are his boots. Jimmy and me can tell you exactly where he is!'

Before they knew it, Kevin had hurried Daisy and Jimmy into his office, leaving the Waymanns and Gary outside.

'OK.' The manager sat them down in two big blue leather armchairs. 'Run that by me again, would you?'

'These are Robbie's boots!' Daisy said again, the evidence nestled safely in her lap. 'Bernie King gave him drugs and kidnapped him. He's brainwashed him and made him sign for Ashby City.'

'Bernie King?' Kevin frowned, as if trying to remember.

'Yeah, the new groundsman,' Jimmy explained. He looked tiny in the outsized armchair, his skinny legs dangling.

'He's an Ashby City spy,' Daisy added. She was beginning to relax. Soon everything would be fine.

'We have to get Robbie back to Highfield,' Jimmy rushed on. 'We need him to be here in time for tomorrow's match.'

'This is serious stuff,' Kevin pointed out. 'You're saying that this King guy has a link with City?'

'He was their groundsman once,' Daisy confirmed, sitting on the edge of the slippery seat. 'He's been giving them lots of stuff about your tactics, using e-mail and everything.'

Kevin stood up, paced up and down, then paused. 'Tell me again, where did you get those boots?'

'In City's changing rooms!' Daisy insisted. 'That's how come we know where Robbie is now!'

'Gotcha!' Kevin nodded, his eyes narrowed, lost in thought.

Then the door opened and Robbie Exley walked in.

Twenty-One

'Eek!' Daisy squeaked.

'Uh!' Jimmy gasped.

'Hey!' Robbie grinned, the blond streaks in his hair gleaming in the evening sun.

'W-w-what…?' Daisy stammered.

'How come?' Jimmy hissed at Daisy.

'These two say you've been kidnapped,' Kevin explained calmly. 'You don't look very kidnapped to me.'

'I'm not,' Robbie assured the Steelers manager. He turned to Jimmy and Daisy. 'What's all this about?'

'Eek!' Daisy said, faintly this time, her head spinning. 'He's Robbie's double!' she muttered to Kevin Crowe. 'Don't trust him. He's an enemy spy!'

Without saying a word. Robbie picked up a ball from the corner of the room and started to juggle it. He balanced it on his right toe, flicked it up on to his chest, let it roll on to his knee, jerked it up on to his head and nodded it towards Daisy.

She caught the ball.

'Still think I'm Robbie's double?' Robbie asked with a grin.

Daisy frowned and shook her head. 'We thought Bernie King had drugged you and brainwashed you,' she muttered in a hollow voice. 'But it looks like we were wrong.'

'Not so much of the "we"!' Jimmy protested, standing up and beginning to back towards the door. 'This was all your idea, remember!'

Daisy's brow creased. 'I don't get this,' she sighed at Robbie. 'Why did you miss training?'

'Ah!' Kevin stepped in. 'That's what this is all about. You knew Robbie didn't show up for training, so you put two and two together and came up with five.'

'So where were you?' Jimmy asked the soccer legend.

'My dad was sick. I had to rush him into hospital,' Robbie explained. 'I didn't have my mobile phone with me, so it was a while before I could get in touch with Kevin.'

'By which time, Robbie's dad was in the high dependency unit, recovering from a heart attack,' Kevin went on. 'I told Robbie to stay there as long as he needed. Luckily the patient is over the worst.'

Daisy listened hard. Her eyebrows shot up under her messy fringe, she looked sideways at Jimmy. 'Uh-oh!' she said through clenched teeth.

Splat! Talk about getting egg on your face. This scrambled mess was a whole omelette!

'But what about these boots?' Jimmy wanted to know. He seized them from Daisy and held them up for Robbie to see.

'Yeah, we found them in City's changing rooms!' Daisy cried, in one last effort to prove her theory. Maybe Robbie had made up the stuff about his dad to fool Kevin. What if he had really signed for City after all?

Robbie studied the boots, then shrugged. 'They do look like mine,' he admitted.

'No, actually, they're mine!' William King announced, walking in without knocking. The young player was followed by his Uncle Bernie, and by Mr and Mrs Waymann. 'They're a copy of yours. I bought them from the local sports shop,' he said to Robbie.

'Eek-eek!' Daisy's mouse noises kept on escaping from her lips.

What's with the eeks? Herbie asked from her top pocket.

'I used the boots for my trial at Low Moor because I thought they'd bring me luck,' William explained. 'City invited me over for their training session earlier this afternoon. I was mega, even if I say it myself!'

'*Eek* – you – *squeak* – played – at – Low – *gurgle* – Moor?' Daisy gasped.

'Yeah, why not?' William retorted. 'I haven't signed a contract for Steelers, so I'm free to go to another club if someone else wants me.'

'It's true,' Kevin confirmed.

Behind his back, Bernie King nodded and smirked.

Eek! Herbie said. *Let's get out of here. Come on, Daisy, va-va-vroom!*

'So you think you did OK?' Robbie asked William chattily, as if Daisy hadn't just made the biggest mistake of her entire life.

William nodded. 'City want me to go to them on loan, starting next season.'

'Nice one,' Robbie said.

'Yeah, William, you deserve a lucky break,' Kevin agreed. Then he turned to Daisy and Jimmy. 'Happy now?' he asked.

Like a big, big boo-boo! A major, major mess! The boots

were copies, exactly like the ones Daisy herself had bought. She groaned and hung her head.

'Don't worry, Mr Crowe, let me deal with Daisy and Jimmy.' Witchy Waymann stepped forward in a cloud of perfume. 'I'll find a suitable punishment.'

'*Herrufff!*' Fat Lennox said, waddling through the half-open door.

'Sorry, I couldn't stop him!' Winona burst in after the dog, then squeezed to the front with her notepad. 'Is it a fact that Robbie is playing for Steelers after all?' she asked Kevin Crowe, her pencil poised. 'If it's true, I can phone the news through to the *Helston Herald* in time for tomorrow morning's paper!'

Wow! Herbie sighed. *I mean, wow!*

'Yeah, wow!' Daisy agreed, snuggling deep into bed.

Waymann wasn't going to punish her and Jimmy, thanks to Super Rob.

'Do me a favour and leave the kids alone,' Robbie had asked the head teacher. 'They only got involved because they care so much about their team. You can't really blame them for that.'

'Hmmm!' Waymann said, breathing hard through her nose.

'Hmph!' Bernie King echoed.

'Tell you what, let Daisy and Jimmy off and come to

the match tomorrow,' Robbie offered. 'You, Bernie and Michael – be my guests!'

'Ohhh!' Waymann had sighed, seeing herself dressed up in her best lilac suit and sitting in the directors' box. 'Really – do you mean it? Oh, that would be wonderful, Robbie – erm – do you mind if I call you Robbie? Wouldn't it, Michael? Wouldn't that be absolutely marvellous – to see the final match of the season from the best seats in the ground?'

'I still don't trust Bernie King!' Daisy muttered now as she settled down to sleep. 'Did you see him sniggering in Kevin's office?'

Yeah, Herbie mumbled sleepily.

Daisy stroked the hamster's bald spot. 'I still think Bernie's a spy,' she muttered.

It was dark. Her dad had already turned off her light. She was supposed to be snoozing.

Don't even go there! Herbie advised. *I've had enough of this spy stuff, OK!*

'Hmm,' Daisy sulked. But she knew, deep down, the hamster was right.

'Come on, the Blues!' Jimmy and Daisy screeched.
Their throats were sore from singing and yelling, Daisy's nails were bitten right down.

'We shall not – we shall not be moved!' Winona and

Nathan sang at the tops of their voices.

Their families sat in the rows behind them, looking down on the smooth green turf of Highfield.

'Come on, the Blues!' Daisy's dad roared. He waved his blue and white scarf, leaped out of his seat, covered his eyes with both hands, groaned and then cheered again.

The score was nil–nil. A neat cross from Lyndon Simons had found Robbie in the goalmouth but the City keeper had made a superb save. City too had had their chances but failed to score.

And now there were only five precious minutes left.

'We're never gonna do it!' Jimmy sighed. He felt like he'd been tossed around like a boat in a storm – up on the crest of a wave one second, then pitching down to the sea bed the next.

'Yes, we are!' Daisy promised him. *We will win!* she chanted to herself. *We will win! We will win!*

'We shall not be moved!' Winona crooned, wafting her Steelers scarf across Nathan's face.

'Marc Predoux was out of position just then,' Nathan pointed out. 'He should have been inside the box to receive that last pass!'

'Shut up, Nathan!' Winona muttered.

Daisy glanced sideways. 'I thought you fancied him?' she whispered to Winona.

'Not any more,' Winona sniffed. She'd phoned her

headline through to the *Herald – Robbie Heads Up Steelers' Attack!* – and she was happy. 'I used to fancy him, Daisy. But not any more. Believe me, Nathan's history!'

'Come on, the Blues!' Jimmy yelped, as Pedro Martinez took the ball on a swift run down the right wing.

They were in the dying minutes. It was now or never.

Robbie was there in the goalmouth, with two City defenders and the goalie. Pedro sent a high pass. Robbie leaped head and shoulders above the rest. With a smooth, graceful move of the head he flicked the ball past the goalkeeper into the back of the net.

'Goal!' sixty thousand people roared.

'One – nil!' Daisy cried, clinging to Jimmy and jumping up and down.

Ouch! Herbie squeaked from deep inside Daisy's pocket. *Did we score?*

'One – nil! One – nil!' the Steelers' fans crowed.

Ashby City hung their heads in defeat. Robbie and Pedro hugged.

'We won!' Daisy yelled as the final whistle blew. 'We're top of the Premiership. We're the champions!'

'Are you blubbing?' Jimmy asked her.

The players did their lap of honour, hands raised above their heads, applauding their supporters.

'Nope!' Daisy fibbed, brushing her wet cheeks with the back of her hand.

'We – are – the – champ-i-ons!' she and Jimmy sang until their lungs burst.

Kevin came out of the dugout and turned to wave at the directors' box. Then he went and joined his team on the pitch.

'We are the champions!' Daisy, Jimmy, Nathan and Winona cried.

Robbie stopped under their box and smiled up at the sea of Steelers fans.

Daisy looked down at her hero. It was the best, the sweetest feeling...to be top of the Premiership, to be part of Steelers' success.